# Guardians of Time

Poul Anderson

# Guardians
# of Time

Pan Books
London and Sydney

*To Kenny Gray –*
*who'll tell me what I did wrong –*
*and to Gloria,*
*who knows better*

First published 1961 by Victor Gollancz Ltd.
This edition published 1964 by Pan Books Ltd,
Cavaye Place, London sw10 9pg
4th printing 1977
© Poul Anderson 1961
ISBN 0 330 01660 1
Printed and bound in Great Britain by
Hunt Barnard Printing Ltd, Aylesbury,
Buckinghamshire

# CONTENTS

## ACKNOWLEDGMENTS

The stories in this book have all appeared (in slightly different form) in *The Magazine of Fantasy and Science Fiction* and are copyright by Mercury Press Inc., as follows:

"Time Patrol", May 1955, copyright 1955
"Brave to be a King", August 1959, copyright 1959
"The Only Game in Town", January 1960, copyright 1960
"Delenda Est", December 1955, copyright 1955

# TIME PATROL

## I

*MEN WANTED—21–40, pref. single, mil. or tech.
exp., good physique, for high-pay work with foreign
travel, Engineering Studies Co., 305 E. 45, 9–12 & 2–6.*

'THE WORK is, you understand, somewhat unusual,' said
Mr Gordon. 'And confidential. I trust you can keep a
secret?'

'Normally,' said Manse Everard. 'Depends on what the
secret is, of course.'

Mr Gordon smiled. It was a curious smile, a closed curve
of his lips which was not quite like any Everard had seen
before. He spoke easy colloquial General American, and
wore an undistinguished business suit, but there was a
foreignness over him which was more than dark complexion,
beardless cheeks and the incongruity of Mongolian eyes
above a thin Caucasian nose. It was hard to place.

'We're not spies, if that's what you're thinking,' he said.

Everard grinned. 'Sorry. Please don't think I've gone as
hysterical as the rest of the country. I've never had access
to confidential data anyway. But your ad mentioned overseas
operations, and the way things are – I'd like to keep my
passport, you understand.'

He was a big man, with blocky shoulders and a slightly
battered face under crew-cut brown hair. His papers lay
before him: Army discharge, the record of work in several
places as a mechanical engineer. Mr Gordon had seemed
barely to glance at them.

The office was ordinary: a desk and a couple of chairs, a
filing cabinet, and a door leading off in the rear. A window
opened on the banging traffic of New York, six stories down.

'Independent spirit,' said the man behind the desk. 'I like
that. So many of them come cringing in, as if they'd be
grateful for a kick. Of course, with your background you

aren't desperate yet. You can still get work, even in . . . ah, I believe the current term is a rolling readjustment.'

'I was interested,' said Everard. 'I've worked abroad, as you can see, and would like to travel again. But, frankly, I still don't have the faintest idea what your outfit does.'

'We do a good many things,' said Mr Gordon. 'Let me see . . . you've been in combat. France and Germany.' Everard blinked; his papers had included a record of medals, but he'd have sworn the man hadn't had time to read them. 'Um . . . would you mind grasping those knobs on the arms of your chair? Thank you. Now, how do you react to physical danger?'

Everard bristled. 'Look here—'

Mr Gordon's eyes flicked to an instrument on his desk: it was merely a box with an indicator needle and a couple of dials. 'Never mind. What are your views on international-ism?'

'Say, now —'

'Communism? Fascism? Women? Your personal ambi-tions? . . . That's all. You don't have to answer.'

'What the devil is this, anyway?' snapped Everard.

'A bit of psychological testing. Forget it. I've no interest in your opinions except as they reflect basic emotional orien-tation.' Mr Gordon leaned back, making a bridge of his fingers. 'Very promising, so far. Now, here's the set-up. We're doing work which is, as I've told you, highly con-fidential. We . . . ah . . . we're planning to spring a surprise on our competitors.' He chuckled. 'Go ahead and report me to the FBI if you wish. We've already been investigated and have a clean bill of health. You'll find that we really do carry on world-wide financial and engineering operations. But there's another aspect of the job, and that's the one we want men for. I'll pay you one hundred dollars to go in the back room and take a set of tests. It'll last about three hours. If you don't pass, that's the end of it. If you do, we'll sign you on, tell you the facts, and start you training. Are you game?'

Everard hesitated. He had a feeling of being rushed. There was more to this enterprise than an office and one bland stranger. Still. . . .

Decision. 'I'll sign on *after* you've told me what it's all about.'

8

'As you wish,' shrugged Mr Gordon. 'Suit yourself. The tests will say whether you're going to or not, you know. We use some very advanced techniques.'

That, at least, was entirely true. Everard knew a little something about modern psychology: encephalographs, association tests, the Minnesota profile. He did not recognize any of the hooded machines that hummed and blinked around him. The questions which the assistant – a white-skinned, completely hairless man of indeterminate age, with a heavy accent and no facial expression – fired at him seemed irrelevant to anything. And what was the metal cap he was supposed to wear on his head? Into what did the wires from it lead?

He stole glances at the meter faces, but the letters and numerals were like nothing he had seen before. Not English, French, Russian, Greek, Chinese, anything belonging to AD 1954. Perhaps he was already beginning to realize the truth, even then.

A curious self-knowledge grew in him as the tests proceeded. Manson Emmert Everard, age 30, one time lieutenant in the US Army Engineers; design and production experience in America, Sweden, Arabia; still a bachelor, though with increasingly wistful thoughts about his married friends; no current girl, no close ties of any kind; a bit of a bibliophile; a dogged poker player; fondness for sailboats and horses and rifles; a camper and fisherman on his vacations. He had known it all, of course, but only as isolated shards of fact. It was peculiar, this sudden sensing of himself as an integrated organism, this realization that each characteristic was a single inevitable facet of an over-all pattern.

He came out exhausted and wringing wet. Mr Gordon offered him a cigarette and swept eyes rapidly over a series of coded sheets which the assistant gave him. Now and then he muttered a phrase: '. . . Zeth–20 cortical . . . undifferentiated evaluation here . . . psychic reaction to antitoxin . . . weakness in central coordination. . . .' He had slipped into an accent, a lilt and a treatment of vowels which were like nothing Everard had heard in a long experience of the ways in which the English language can be mangled.

It was half an hour before he looked up again. Everard was getting restless, a faint anger stirring at this cavalier treatment, but interest kept him sitting quietly. Mr Gordon flashed improbably white teeth in a broad, satisfied grin. 'Ah. At last. Do you know, I've had to reject twenty-four candidates already? But you'll do. You'll definitely do.'

'Do for what?' Everard leaned forward, conscious of his pulse picking up.

'The Patrol. You're going to be a kind of policeman.'

'Yeh? Where?'

'Everywhere. And everywhen. Brace yourself, this is going to be a shock.

'You see, our company, while legitimate enough, is only a front and a source of funds. Our real business is patrolling time.'

## 2

The Academy was in the American West. It was also in the Oligocene period, a warm age of forests and grasslands when man's ratty ancestors scuttled away from the tread of giant mammals. It had been built a thousand years ago; it would be maintained for half a million – long enough to graduate as many as the Time Patrol would require – and then be carefully demolished so that no trace would remain. Later the glaciers would come, and there would be men, and in the, year AD 19352 (the 7841st year of the Morennian Triumph) these men would find a way to travel through time and return to the Oligocene to establish the Academy.

It was a complex of long, low buildings, smooth curves and shifting colours, spreading over a greensward between enormous ancient trees. Beyond it, hills and woods rolled off to a great brown river, and at night you could sometimes hear the bellowing of titanotheres or the distant squall of a sabre-tooth.

Everard stepped out of the time shuttle – a big, featureless metal box – with a dryness in his throat. It felt like his first day in the Army, twelve years ago – or fifteen to twenty million years in the future, if you preferred – lonely and helpless, and wishing desperately for some honourable way to go home. It was small comfort to see the other shuttles discharging a total of fifty-odd young men and women. The recruits moved slowly together, forming an awkward clump.

They didn't speak at first, but stood staring at each other. Everard recognized a Hoover collar and a bowler; the styles of dress and hairdo moved up through 1954 and on. Where was she from, the girl with the iridescent, close-fitting culottes and the green lipstick and the fantastically waved yellow hair? No . . . when?

A man of about twenty-five happened to stand beside him; obviously British, from the threadbare tweeds and the long, thin face. He seemed to be hiding a truculent bitterness under his mannered exterior. 'Hello,' said Everard. 'Might as well get acquainted.' He gave his name and origin.

'Charles Whitcomb, London, 1947,' said the other shyly. 'I was just demobbed – RAF – and this looked like a good chance. Now I wonder.'

'It may be,' said Everard, thinking of the salary. Fifteen thousand a year to start with! How did they figure years, though. Must be in terms of one's actual duration-sense.

A man strolled in their direction. He was a slender young fellow in a skin-tight grey uniform with a deep-blue cloak which seemed to twinkle, as if it had stars sewn in. His face was pleasant, smiling, and he spoke genially with a neutral accent: 'Hello, there! Welcome to the Academy. I take it you all know English?' Everard noticed a man in the shabby remnants of a German uniform, and a Hindu, and others who were probably from several foreign countries.

'We'll use English, then, till you've all learned Temporal.' The man lounged easily, hands on his hips. 'My name is Dard Kelm. I was born in – let me see – 9573 Christian reckoning, but I've made a speciality of your period. Which, by the way, extends from 1850 to 1975, though you're all from some in-between years. I'm your official wailing wall, if something goes wrong.

'This place is run along different lines from what you've probably been expecting. We don't turn out men en masse, so the elaborate discipline of a classroom or an army is not required. Each of you will have individual as well as general instruction. We don't need to punish failure in studies, because the preliminary tests have guaranteed there won't be any and made the chance of failure on the job small. Each of you has a high maturity rating in terms of your particular cultures. However, the variation in aptitudes means that if we're to develop each individual to the fullest, there must be personal guidance.

'There's little formality here beyond normal courtesy. You'll have chances for recreation as well as study. We never expect more of you than you can give. I might add that the hunting and fishing are still pretty good even in this neighbourhood, and if you fly just a few hundred miles they're fantastic.

'Now, if there aren't any questions, please follow me and I'll get you settled.'

Dard Kelm demonstrated the gadgets in a typical room. They were the sort you would have expected by, say, AD 2000: unobtrusive furniture readily adjusted to a perfect fit, refresher cabinets, screens which could draw on a huge library of recorded sight and sound for entertainment. Nothing too advanced, as yet. Each cadet had his own room in the 'dormitory' building; meals were in a central refectory, but arrangements could be made for private parties. Everard felt the tension easing within him.

A welcoming banquet was held. The courses were familiar, but the silent machines which rolled up to serve them were not. There was wine, beer, an ample supply of tobacco. Maybe something had been slipped into the food, for Everard felt as euphoric as the others. He ended up beating out boogie on a piano while half a dozen people made the air hideous with attempts at song.

Only Charles Whitcomb held back. Sipping a moody glass over in a corner by himself, Dard Kelm was tactful and did not try to force him into joining.

Everard decided he was going to like it. But the work and the organization and the purpose were still shadows.

'Time travel was discovered at a period when the Chorite Heresiarchy was breaking up,' said Kelm, in the lecture hall. 'You'll study the details later; for now, take my word that it was a turbulent age, when commercial and genetic rivalry was a tooth-and-claw matter between giant combines, anything went, and the various governments were pawns in a galactic game. The time effect was the by-product of a search for a means of instantaneous transportation, which some of you will realize requires infinitely discontinuous functions for its mathematical description ... as does travel into the past. I won't go into the theory of it – you'll get some of that in the physics classes – but merely state that it involves the concept of infinite-valued relationships in a continuum of 4N dimensions, where N is the total number of particles in the universe.

'Naturally, the group which discovered this, the Nine, were aware of the possibilities. Not only commercial – trading, mining, and other enterprises you can readily imagine – but the chance of striking a death-blow at their enemies. You see, time is variable; the past can be changed —'

'Question!' It was the girl from 1972, Elizabeth Gray, who was a rising young physicist in her own period.

'Yes?' said Kelm politely.

'I think you're describing a logically impossible situation. I'll grant the possibility of time travel, seeing that we're here, but an event cannot both *have* happened and *not* have happened. That's self-contradictory.'

'Only if you insist on a logic which is not Aleph-sub-Aleph-valued,' said Kelm. 'What happens is like this: suppose I went back in time and prevented your father from meeting your mother. You would never have been born. That portion of universal history would read differently; it would always have been different, though I would retain memory of the "original" state of affairs.'

'Well, how about doing the same to yourself?' asked Elizabeth. 'Would you cease existing?'

'No, because I would belong to the section of history prior to my own intervention. Let's apply it to you. If you went back to, I would guess, 1946, and worked to prevent your parents' marriage in 1947, you would still have existed in that year; you would not go out of existence just because you had influenced events. The same would apply even if you had only been in 1946 one microsecond before shooting the man who would otherwise have become your father.'

'But then I'd exist without – without an origin!' she protested. 'I'd have life, and memories, and ... everything ... though *nothing* had produced them."

Kelm shrugged. 'What of it? You insist that the causal law, or strictly speaking the conservation-of-energy law, involves only continuous functions. Actually, discontinuity is entirely possible.'

He laughed and leaned on the lectern. 'Of course, there are impossibilities,' he said. 'You could not be your own mother, for instance, because of sheer genetics. If you went back and married your former father, the children would be different, none of them you, because each would have only half your chromosomes.'

Clearing his throat: 'Let's not stray from the subject. You'll learn the details in other classes. I'm only giving you a general background. To continue: the Nine saw the possibility of going back in time and preventing their enemies from ever having got started, even from ever being born. But then the Danellians appeared.'

For the first time, his casual, half-humorous air dropped, and he stood there as a man in the presence of the unknowable. He spoke quietly: 'The Danellians are part of the future – our future, more than a million years ahead of me. Man has evolved into something . . . impossible to describe. You'll probably never meet a Danellian. If you ever should, it will be . . . rather a shock. They aren't malignant – nor benevolent – they are as far beyond anything we can know or feel as we are beyond those insectivores who are going to be our ancestors. It isn't good to meet that sort of thing face to face.

'They were simply concerned with protecting their own existence. Time travel was old when they emerged, there had been uncountable opportunities for the foolish and the greedy and the mad to go back and turn history inside out. They did not wish to forbid the travel – it was part of the complex which had led to them – but they had to regulate it. The Nine were prevented from carrying out their schemes. And the Patrol was set up to police the time lanes.

'Your work will be mostly within your own eras, unless you graduate to unattached status. You will live, on the whole, ordinary lives, family and friends as usual; the secret part of those lives will have the satisfactions of good pay, protection, occasional vacations in some very interesting places, supremely worthwhile work. But you will always be on call. Sometimes you will help time travellers who have got into difficulties, one way or another. Sometimes you will work on missions, the apprehension of would-be political or military or economic conquistadors. Sometimes the Patrol will accept damage as done, and work instead to set up counteracting influences in later periods which will swing history back to the desired track.

'I wish all of you luck.'

The first part of instruction was physical and psychological. Everard had never realized how his own life had crippled him, in body and mind; he was only half the man he could be. It came hard, but in the end it was a joy to feel the utterly controlled power of muscles, the emotions which had grown deeper for being disciplined, the swiftness and precision of conscious thought.

Somewhere along the line he was thoroughly conditioned against revealing anything about the Patrol, even hinting at its existence, to any unauthorized person. It was simply impossible for him to do so, under any influence; as impossible as jumping to the moon. He also learned the ins and outs of his twentieth-century public *persona*.

Temporal, the artificial language with which Patrolmen from all ages could communicate without being understood by strangers, was a miracle of logically organized expressiveness.

He thought he knew something about combat, but he had to learn the tricks and the weapons of fifty thousand years, all the way from a Bronze Age rapier to a cyclic blast which could annihilate a continent. Returned to his own era, he would be given a limited arsenal, but he might be called into other periods and overt anachronism was rarely permissible.

There was the study of history, science, arts and philosophies, fine details of dialect and mannerism. These last were only for the 1850–1975 period; if he had occasion to go elsewhen he would pick up special instruction from a hypnotic conditioner. It was such machines that made it possible to complete his training in three months.

He learned the organization of the Patrol. Up 'ahead' lay the mystery which was Danellian civilization, but there was little direct contact with it. The Patrol was set up in semimilitary fashion, with ranks, though without special formalities. History was divided into milieux, with a head office located in a major city for a selected twenty-year period (disguised by some ostensible activity such as commerce) and various branch offices. For his time, there were three milieux: the Western world, headquarters in London; Russia, in Moscow; Asia, in Peiping; each in the easy-going years 1890-1910, when concealment was less difficult than in later decades, when there were smaller offices such as Gordon's. An ordinary attached agent lived as usual in his own time, often with an authentic job. Communication between years was by tiny robot shuttles or by courier, with automatic shunts to keep such messages from piling up at one instant.

The entire organization was so vast that he could not really appreciate the fact. He had entered something new and exciting, that was all he truly grasped with all layers of consciousness . . . as yet.

He found his instructors friendly, ready to gab. The grizzled veteran who taught him to handle spaceships had fought in the Martian war of 3890. 'You boys catch on fairly quick,' he said. 'It's hell, though, teaching pre-industrial people. We've quit even trying to give them more than the rudiments. Had a Roman here once – Caesar's time – fairly bright boy, too, but he never got it through his head that a machine can't be treated like a horse. As for those Babylonians, time travel just wasn't in their world-picture. We had to give them a battle-of-the-gods routine.'

'What routine are you giving us?' asked Whitcomb.

The spaceman regarded him narrowly. 'The truth,' he said at last. 'As much of it as you can take.'

'How did you get into this job?'

'Oh . . . I was shot up off Jupiter. Not much left of me. They picked me up, built me a new body – since none of my people were alive, and I was presumed dead, there didn't seem much point in going back home. No fun living under the Guidance Corps. So I took this position here. Good company, easy living, and furloughs in a lot of eras.' The spaceman grinned. 'Wait till you've been to the decadent stage of the Third Matriarchy! You don't know what fun is.'

Everard said nothing. He was too captured by the spectacle of Earth, rolling enormous against the stars.

He made friends with his fellow cadets. They were a congenial bunch – naturally, with the same type being picked for

Patrollers, bold and intelligent minds. There were a couple of romances. No *Portrait of Jenny* stuff: marriage was entirely possible, with the couple picking some year in which to set up housekeeping. He himself liked the girls, but kept his head.

Oddly, it was the silent and morose Whitcomb with whom he struck up the closest friendship. There was something appealing about the Englishman; he was so cultured, such a thoroughly good fellow, and still somehow lost.

They were out riding one day, on horses whose remote ancestors scampered before their gigantic descendants. Everard had a rifle, in the hope of bagging a shovel-tusker he had seen. Both wore Academy uniform, light greys which were cool and silky under the hot yellow sun.

'I wonder we're allowed to hunt,' remarked the American. 'Suppose I shoot a sabretooth – in Asia, I suppose – which was originally slated to eat one of those prehuman insectivores. Won't that change the whole future?'

'No,' said Whitcomb. He had progressed faster in studying the theory of time travel. 'You see, it's rather as if the continuum were a mesh of tough rubber bands. It isn't easy to distort it; the tendency is always for it to snap back to its, uh, "former" shape. One individual insectivore doesn't matter, it's the total genetic pool of their species which led to man.

'Likewise, if I killed a sheep in the Middle Ages, I wouldn't wipe out all its later descendants, maybe all the sheep there were by 1940. Rather, those would still be there, unchanged down to their very genes in spite of a different ancestry, because over so long a period of time all the sheep, or men, are descendants of *all* the earlier sheep or men. Compensation don't you see; somewhere along the line, some other ancestor supplies the genes you thought you had eliminated.

'In the same way . . . oh, suppose I went back and prevented Booth from killing Lincoln. Unless I took very elaborate precautions, it would probably happen that someone else did the shooting and Booth got blamed anyway.

'That resilience of time is the reason travel is permitted at all. If you want to change things, you have to go about it just right and work very hard, usually.'

His mouth twisted. 'Indoctrination! We're told again and again that if *we* interfere, there's going to be punishment for us. I'm not allowed to go back and shoot that ruddy bastard Hitler in his cradle. I'm supposed to let him grow up as he did, and start the war, and kill my girl.'

Everard rode quietly for a while. The only noise was the squeak of saddle leather and the rustle of long grass. 'Oh,' he said at last. 'I'm sorry. Want to talk about it?'

'Yes. I do. But there isn't much. She was in the WAAF – Mary Nelson – we were going to get married after the war. She was in London in '44. November seventeenth, I'll never forget that date. The V-bombs got her. She'd gone over to a neighbour's house in Streatham – was on leave, you see, staying with her mother. That house was blown up; her own home wasn't scratched.'

Whitcomb's cheeks were bloodless. He stared emptily before him. 'It's going to be jolly hard not to . . . not to go back, just a few years, and see her at the very least. Only see her again. . . . No! I don't dare.'

Everard laid a hand on the man's shoulder, awkwardly, and they rode on in silence.

The class moved ahead, each at his own pace, but there was enough compensation so that all graduated together: a brief ceremony followed by a huge party and many maudlin arrangements for later reunions. Then each went back to the same year he had come from: the same hour.

Everard accepted Gordon's congratulations, got a list of contemporary agents (several of them holding jobs in places like military intelligence), and returned to his apartment. Later he might find work arranged for him in some sensitive listening post, but his present assignment – for income-tax purposes, 'special consultant to Engineering Studies Co.' – was only to read a dozen papers a day for the indications of time travel he had been taught to spot, and hold himself ready for a call.

As it happened, he made his own first job.

3

It was a peculiar feeling to read the headlines and know, more or less, what was coming next. It took the edge off, but added a sadness, for this was a tragic era. He could sympathize with Whitcomb's desire to go back and change history.

Only, of course, one man was too limited. He could not change it for the better, except by some freak; most likely he would bungle everything. Go back and kill Hitler and the Japanese and Soviet leaders – maybe someone shrewder would take their place. Maybe atomic energy would lie fallow, and the glorious flowering of the Venusian Renaissance never happen. The devil we know. . . .

He looked out of his window. Lights flamed against a hectic sky; the street crawled with automobiles and a hurrying, faceless crowd; he could not see the towers of Manhattan from here, but he knew they reared arrogant towards the clouds. And it was all one swirl on a river that swept from the peaceful prehuman landscape where he had been to the unimaginable Danellian future. How many billions and trillions of human creatures lived, laughed, wept, worked, hoped, and died in its currents!

Well. . . . He sighed, stoked his pipe, and turned back. A long walk had not made him less restless; his mind and body were impatient for something to do. But it was late and . . . He went over to the bookshelf, picked out a volume more or less at random, and started to read. It was a collection of Victorian and Edwardian stories.

A passing reference struck him. Something about a tragedy at Addleton and the singular contents of an ancient British barrow. Nothing more. Hm. Time travel? He smiled to himself.

Still. . . .

*No,* he thought. *This is crazy.*

It wouldn't do any harm to check up, though. The incident was mentioned as occurring in the year 1894, in England. He could get out back files of the London *Times.* Nothing else to do. . . . Probably that was why he was stuck with this dull newspaper assignment: so that his mind, grown nervous from boredom, would prowl into every conceivable corner.

He was on the steps of the public library as it opened.

The account was there, dated June 25, 1894, and several days following. Addleton was a village in Kent, distinguished chiefly by a Jacobean estate belonging to Lord Wyndham and a barrow of unknown age. The nobleman, an enthusiastic amateur archaeologist, had been excavating it, together with one James Rotherhithe, an expert from the British Museum who happened to be a relative. Lord Wyndham had uncovered a rather meagre burial chamber: a few artifacts nearly rusted and rotted away, bones of men and horses. There was also a chest in surprisingly good condition, containing ingots of an unknown metal presumed to be a lead or silver alloy. He fell deathly ill, with symptoms of a peculiarly lethal poisoning; Rotherhithe, who had barely looked into the casket, was not affected, and circumstantial evidence suggested that he had slipped the nobleman a dose of some obscure Asiatic concoction. Scotland Yard arrested the man when Lord Wyndham died, on the twenty-fifth. Rotherhithe's family engaged the services of a well-known private detective, who was able to show, by most ingenious reasoning, followed by tests on animals, that the accused was innocent and that a 'deadly emanation' from the chest was responsible. Box and contents had been thrown into the English Channel. Congratulations all round. Fade-out to happy ending.

Everard sat quietly in the long, hushed room. The story didn't tell enough. But it was highly suggestive, to say the least.

Then why hadn't the Victorian office of the Patrol investigated? Or had they? Probably. They wouldn't advertise their results, of course.

Still, he'd better send a memorandum.

Returning to his apartment, he took one of the little message shuttles given him, laid a report in it, and set the control studs for the London office, June 25, 1894. When he pushed the final button the box vanished with a small whoosh of air rushing in where it had been.

It returned in a few minutes. Everard opened it and took out a sheet of foolscap covered with neat typing – yes, the typewriter had been invented by then, of course. He scanned it with the swiftness he had learned.

'Dear Sir:

'In reply to yrs. of September 6, 1954, beg to acknowledge receipt and would commend your diligence. The affair has only just begun at this end, and we are much occupied at present with preventing assassination of Her Majesty, as well

20

as with the Balkan Question, the 1890–22370 opium trade with China, &c. While we can, of course, settle current business and then return to this, it is well to avoid *curiosa* such as being in two places at once, which might be noticed. Would therefore much appreciate it if you and some qualified British agent could come to our assistance. Unless we hear otherwise, we shall expect you at 14-B, Old Osborne Road, on June 26, 1894, at 12 midnight. Believe me, Sir, yr. humble & obt. svt.,

J. Mainwethering'

There followed a note of the spatio-temporal coordinates, incongruous under all that floridness.

Everard called up Gordon, got an okay, and arranged to pick up a time hopper at the 'company's' warehouse. Then he shot a note to Charlie Whitcomb in 1947, got a one-word reply – 'Surely' – and went off to get his machine.

It was reminiscent of a motorcycle without wheels or handlebars. There were two saddles and an antigravity propulsion unit. Everard set the dials for Whitcomb's era, touched the main button, and found himself in another warehouse.

London, 1947. He sat for a moment, reflecting that at this instant he himself, seven years younger, was attending college back in the States. Then Whitcomb shouldered past the watchman and took his hand. 'Good to see you again, old chap,' he said. His haggard face lit up in the curiously charming smile which Everard had come to know. 'And so Victoria, eh?'

'Reckon so. Jump on.' Everard reset. This time he would emerge in an office. A very private inner office.

It blinked into existence around him. There was an unexpectedly heavy effect to the oak furniture, the thick carpet, the flaring gas mantles. Electric lights were available, but Dalhousie & Roberts was a solid, conservative import house. Mainwethering himself got out of a chair and came to greet them: a large and pompous man with bushy side whiskers and a monocle. But he had also an air of strength, and an Oxford accent so cultivated that Everard could hardly understand it.

'Good evening, gentlemen. Pleasant journey, I trust? Oh,

yes . . . sorry . . . you gentlemen are new to the business, eh, what? Always a bit disconcerting at first. I remember how shocked I was on a visit to the twenty-first century. Not British at all. . . . Only a *res naturae,* though, only another facet of an always surprising universe, eh? You must excuse my lack of hospitality, but we really are frightfully busy. Fanatic German up in 1917 learned the time-travel secret from an unwary anthropologist, stole a machine, has come to London to assassinate Her Majesty. We're having the devil's own time finding him.'

'Will you?' asked Whitcomb.

'Oh, yes. But deuced hard work, gentlemen, especially when we must operate secretly. I'd like to engage a private inquiry agent, but the only worth while one is entirely too clever. He operates on the principle that when one has eliminated the impossible, whatever remains, however improbable, must be the truth. And time trafficking may not be too improbable for him.'

'I'll bet he's the same man who's working on the Addleton case, or will be tomorrow,' said Everard. 'That isn't important; we know he'll prove Rotherhithe's innocence. What matters is the strong probability that there's been hanky-panky going on back in ancient British times.'

'Saxon, you mean,' corrected Whitcomb, who had checked on the data himself. 'Good many people confuse British and Saxon.'

'Almost as many as confuse Saxons and Jutes,' said Main-wethering blandly. 'Kent was invaded from Jutland, I understand. . . . Ah. Hm. Clothes here, gentlemen. And funds. And papers, all prepared for you. I sometimes think you field agents don't appreciate how much work we have to do in the offices for even the smallest operation. Haw! Pardon. Have you a plan of campaign?'

'Yes.' Everard began stripping off his twentieth-century garments. 'I think so. We both know enough about the Victorian era to get by. I'll have to remain American, though . . . yes, I see you put that in my papers.'

Mainwethering looked mournful. 'If the barrow incident has got into a famous piece of literature as you say, we will be getting a hundred memoranda about it. Yours happened to come first. Two others have arrived since, from 1923 and

1960. Dear me, how I wish I were allowed a robot secretary!'

Everard struggled with the awkward suit. It fitted him well enough, his measurements were on file in this office, but he hadn't appreciated the relative comfort of his own fashions before. Damm that waistcoat! 'Look here,' he said, 'this business may be quite harmless. In fact, since we're here now, it must have *been* harmless. Eh?'

'As of now,' said Mainwethering. 'But consider. You two gentlemen go back to Jutish times and find the marauder. But you fail. Perhaps he shoots you before you can shoot him; perhaps he waylays those we send after you. Then he goes on to establish an industrial revolution or whatever he's after. History changes. You, being back there before the change-point, still exist . . . if only as cadavers . . . but we up here have never been. This conversation never took place. As Horace puts it —'

'Never mind!' laughed Whitcomb. 'We'll investigate the barrow first, in this year, then pop back here and decide what's next.' He bent over and began transferring equipment from a twentieth-century handbag to a Gladstonian monstrosity of flowered cloth. A couple of guns, some physical and chemical apparatus which his own age had not invented, a tiny radio with which to call up the office in case of trouble.

Mainwethering consulted his Bradshaw. 'You can get the 8.23 out of Charing Cross tomorrow morning,' he said. 'Allow half an hour to get from here to the station.'

'Okay.' Everard and Whitcomb remounted their hopper and vanished. Mainwethering sighed, yawned, left instructions with his clerk, and went home. At 7.45 am the clerk was there when the hopper materialized.

4

This was the first moment that the reality of time travel struck home to Everard. He had known it with the top of his mind, been duly impressed, but it was, for his emotions, merely exotic. Now, clopping through a London he did not know in a hansom cab (not a tourist-trap anachronism, but a working machine, dusty and battered); smelling an air which held more smoke than a twentieth-century city but no gasoline fumes; seeing the crowds which milled past – gentlemen in bowlers and top hats, sooty navvies, long-skirted women, and not actors but real, talking, perspiring, laughing and sombre human beings off on real business – it hit him with full force that he was *here*. At this moment his mother had not been born; his grandparents were young couples just getting settled to harness; Grover Cleveland was President of the United States and Victoria was Queen of England; Kipling was writing and the last Indian uprisings in America had yet to come. . . . It was like a blow on the head.

Whitcomb took it more calmly, but his eyes were never still as he watched this day of England's glory. 'I begin to understand,' he murmured. 'They never have agreed whether this was a period of unnatural, stuffy convention and thinly veneered brutality, or the last flower of Western civilization before it started going to seed. Just seeing these people makes me realize: it was everything they have said about it, good and bad, because it wasn't a simple thing happening to everyone, but millions of individual lives.'

'Sure,' said Everard. 'That must be true of every age.'

The train was almost familiar, not very different from the carriages of British Railways anno 1954, which gave Whitcomb occasion for sardonic remarks about inviolable traditions. In a couple of hours it let them off at a sleepy village station among carefully tended flower gardens, where they engaged a buggy to drive them to the Wyndham estate.

A polite constable admitted them after a few questions. They were passing themselves off as archaeologists, Everard from America and Whitcomb from Australia, who had been quite anxious to meet Lord Wyndham and were shocked by his tragic end. Mainwethering, who seemed to have tentacles everywhere, had supplied them with letters of introduction from a well-known authority at the British Museum. The inspector from Scotland Yard agreed to let them look at the barrow – 'the case is solved, gentlemen, there are no more clues, even if my colleague does not agree, hah, hah!' The private agent smiled sourly and watched them with a narrow eye as they approached the mound; he was tall, thin, hawk-faced, and accompanied by a burly, moustached fellow with a limp who seemed a kind of amanuensis.

The barrow was long and high, covered with grass save where a raw scar showed excavation to the funeral chamber.

This had been lined with rough-hewn timbers but had long ago collapsed; fragments of what had been wood still lay on the dirt. 'The newspapers mentioned something about a metal casket,' said Everard. 'I wonder if we might have a look at it too?'

The inspector nodded agreeably and led them off to an outbuilding where the major finds were laid forth on a table. Except for the box, they were only fragments of corroded metal and crumbled bone.

'Hm,' said Whitcomb. His gaze was thoughtful on the sleek, bare face of the small chest. It shimmered bluely, some time-proof alloy yet to be discovered. 'Most unusual. Not primitive at all. You'd almost think it had been machined, eh?'

Everard approached it warily. He had a pretty good idea of what was inside, and all the caution about such matters natural to a citizen of the *soi-disant* Atomic Age. Pulling a counter out of his bag, he aimed it at the box. Its needle wavered, not much but . . .

'Interesting item there,' said the inspector. 'May I ask what it is?'

'An experimental electroscope,' lied Everard. Carefully, he threw back the lid and held the counter above the box.

God! There was enough radioactivity inside to kill a man in a day! He had just a glimpse of heavy, dull-shining ingots before he slammed the lid down again. 'Be careful with that stuff,' he said shakily. Praise heaven, whoever carried that devil's load had come from an age when they knew how to block off radiation!

The private detective had come up behind them, noiselessly. A hunter's look grew on his keen face. 'So you recognize the contents, sir?' he asked quietly.

'Yes. I think so.' Everard remembered that Becquerel would not discover radioactivity for almost two years; even X-rays were still more than a year in the future. He had to be cautious. 'That is . . . in Indian territory I've heard stories about an ore like this which is poisonous —'

'*Most* interesting.' The detective began to stuff a big-bowled pipe. 'Like mercury vapour, what?'

'So Rotherhithe placed that box in the grave, did he?' muttered the inspector.

'Don't be ridiculous!' snapped the detective. 'I have three lines of conclusive proof that Rotherhithe is entirely innocent. What puzzled me was the actual cause of his lordship's death. But if, as this gentleman says, there happened to be a deadly poison buried in that mound ... to discourage grave-robbers? I wonder, though, how the old Saxons came by an American mineral. Perhaps there is something to these theories about early Phoenician voyages across the Atlantic. I have done a little research on a notion of mine that there are Chaldean elements in the Cymric language, and this seems to bear me out.'

Everard felt guilty about what he was doing to the science of archaeology. Oh, well, this box was going to be dumped in the Channel and forgotten. He and Whitcomb made an excuse to leave as soon as possible.

On the way back to London, when they were safely alone in their compartment, the Englishman took out a mouldering fragment of wood. 'Slipped this into my pocket at the barrow,' he said. 'It'll help us date the thing. Hand me that radiocarbon counter, will you?' He popped the wood into the device, turned some knobs, and read off the answer. 'One thousand, four hundred and thirty years, plus or minus about ten. The mound went up around ... um ... AD 464, then, when the Jutes were just getting established in Kent.'

'If those ingots are still that hellish after so long,' murmured Everard, 'I wonder what they were like originally. Hard to see how you could have that much activity with such a long half-life, but then, up in the future they can do things with the atom my period hasn't dreamed of.'

Turning in their report to Mainwethering, they spent a day sight-seeing while he sent messages across time and activated the great machine of the Patrol. Everard was interested in Victorian London, almost captivated in spite of the grime and poverty. Whitcomb got a faraway look in his eyes. 'I'd like to have lived here,' he said.

'Yeah? With their medicine and dentistry?'

'And no bombs falling.' Whitcomb's answer held a defiance.

Mainwethering had arrangements made when they returned to his office. Puffing a cigar, he strode up and down, pudgy hands clasped behind his tailcoat, and rattled off the story.

'Metal been identified with high probability. Isotopic fuel from around the thirtieth century. Checkup reveals that a merchant from the Ing Empire was visiting year 2987 to barter his raw materials for their synthrope, secret of which had been lost in the Interregnum. Naturally, he took precautions, tried to pass himself off as a trader from the Saturnian System, but nevertheless disappeared. So did his time shuttle. Presumably someone in 2987 found out what he was and murdered him for his machine. Patrol notified, but no trace of machine. Finally recovered from fifth-century England by two Patrolmen named, haw! Everard and Whitcomb.'

'If we've already succeeded, why bother?' grinned the American.

Mainwethering looked shocked. 'But my dear fellow! You have not already succeeded. The job is yet to do, in terms of your and my duration-sense. And please do not take success for granted merely because history records it. Time is not rigid; man has free will. If you fail, history will change and will not ever have recorded your success; I will not have told you about it. That is undoubtedly what happened, if I may use the term "happened", in the few cases where the Patrol has a record of failure. Those cases are still being worked on, and if success is achieved at last, history will be changed and there will "always" have been success. *Tempus non nascitur, fit*, if I may indulge in a slight parody.'

'All right, all right, I was only joking,' said Everard. 'Let's get going. *Tempus fugit*.' He added an extra 'g' with malice aforethought, and Mainwethering winced.

It turned out that even the Patrol knew little about the dark period when the Romans had left Britain, the Romano-British civilization was crumbling, and the English were moving in. It had never seemed an important one. The office at London, AD 1000, sent up what material it had, together with suits of clothes that would get by. Everard and Whitcomb spent an hour unconscious under the hypnotic educators, to emerge with fluency in Latin and in several Saxon and Jutish dialects, and with a fair knowledge of the mores.

The clothes were awkward: trousers, shirts, and coats of rough wool, leather cloaks, an interminable collection of thongs and laces. Long flaxen wigs covered modern hair-cuts; a clean shave would pass unnoticed, even in the fifth century. Whitcomb carried an axe, Everard a sword, both made to measure of high-carbon steel, but put more reliance on the little twenty-sixth-century sonic stun guns tucked under their coats. Armour had not been included, but the time hopper had a pair of motorcycle crash helmets in one saddlebag: these would not attract much attention in an age of home-made equipment, and were a good deal stronger and more comfortable than the real thing. They also stowed away a picnic lunch and some earthenware jugs full of good Victorian ale.

'Excellent.' Mainwethering pulled a watch out of his pocket and consulted it. 'I shall expect you back here at . . . shall we say four o'clock? I will have some armed guards on hand, in case you have a prisoner along, and we can go out to tea afterwards.' He shook their hands. 'Good hunting!'

Everard swung on to the time hopper, set the controls for AD 464 at Addleton Barrow, a summer midnight, and threw the switch.

## 5

There was a full moon. Under it, the land lay big and lonely, with a darkness of forest blocking out the horizon. Somewhere a wolf howled. The mound was there yet; they had come late.

Rising on the antigravity unit, they peered across a dense, shadowy wood. A thorp lay about a mile from the barrow, one hall of hewn timber and a cluster of smaller buildings around a courtyard. In the drenching moonlight, it was very quiet.

'Cultivated fields,' observed Whitcomb. His voice was hushed in the stillness. 'The Jutes and Saxons were mostly yeomen, you know, who came here looking for land. Imagine the Britons were pretty well cleared out of this area some years ago.'

'We've got to find out about that burial,' said Everard. 'Shall we go back and locate the moment the grave was made? No, it might be safer to inquire now, at a later date when whatever excitement there was has died down. Say tomorrow morning.'

Whitcomb nodded, and Everard brought the hopper down into the concealment of a thicket and jumped up five hours. The sun was blinding in the north-east, dew glistened on the long grass, and the birds were making an unholy racket. Dismounting, the agents sent the hopper shooting up at fantastic velocity, to hover ten miles above ground and come to them when called on a midget radio built into their helmets.

They approached the thorp openly, whacking off the savage-looking dogs which came snarling at them with the flat of sword and axe. Entering the courtyard, they found it unpaved but richly carpeted with mud and manure. A couple of naked, tow-headed children gaped at them from a hut of earth and wattles. A girl who was sitting outside milking a scrubby little cow let out a small shriek; a thick-built low-browed farmhand swilling the pigs grabbed for a spear. Wrinkling his nose, Everard wished that some of the 'Noble Nordic' enthusiasts of his century could visit this one.

A grey-bearded man with an axe in his hand appeared in the hall entrance. Like everyone else of this period, he was several inches shorter than the twentieth-century average. He studied them warily before wishing them good morning.

Everard smiled politely. 'I hight Uffa Hundingsson, and my brother is Knubbi,' he said. 'We are merchants from Jutland, come hither to trade at Canterbury.' (He gave it the present name, Cant-wara-byrig.) 'Wandering from the place where our ship is beached, we lost our way, and after fumbling about all night found your home.'

'I hight Wulfnoth, son of Aelfred,' said the yeoman. 'Enter and break your fast with us.'

The hall was big and dim and smoky, full of a chattering crowd: Wulfnoth's children, their spouses and children, dependent carls and *their* wives and children and grandchildren. Breakfast consisted of great wooden trenchers of half-cooked pork, washed down by horns of thin sour beer. It was not hard to get a conversation going; these people were as gossipy as isolated yokels anywhere. The trouble was with inventing plausible accounts of what was going on in Jutland. Once or twice Wulfnoth, who was no fool, caught them in some mistake, but Everard said firmly: 'You have heard a falsehood. News takes strange forms when it crosses

29

the sea.' He was surprised to learn how much contact there still was with the old countries. But the talk of weather and crops was not very different from the kind he knew in the twentieth-century Middle West.

Only later was he able to slip in a question about the barrow. Wulfnoth frowned, and his plump, toothless wife hastily made a protective sign towards a rude wooden idol. 'It is not good to speak of such things,' muttered the Jute. 'I would the wizard had not been buried on my land. But he was close to my father, who died last year and would hear of naught else.'

'Wizard?' Whitcomb pricked up his ears. 'What tale is this?'

'Well, you may as well know,' grumbled Wulfnoth. 'He was a stranger hight Stane, who appeared in Canterbury some six years ago. He must have been from far away, for he spoke not the English or British tongues, but King Hengist guested him and eftsoons he learned. He gave the king strange but goodly gifts, and was a crafty redesman, on whom the king came more and more to lean. None dared cross him, for he had a wand which threw thunderbolts and had been seen to cleave rocks and once, in battle with the Britons, burn men down. There are those who thought he was Woden, but that cannot be since he died.'

'Ah, so.' Everard felt a tingle of eagerness. 'And what did he whilst yet he lived?'

'Oh . . . he gave the king wise redes, as I have said. It was his thought that we of Kent should cease thrusting back the Britons and calling in ever more of our kinsmen from the old country; rather, we should make peace with the natives. He thought that with our strength and their Roman learning, we could together shape a mighty realm. He may have been right, though I for one see little use in all these books and baths, to say naught of that weird cross-god they have. . . . Well, anyhow, he was slain by unknowns three years ago, and buried here with sacrifices and such of his possessions as his foes had not reaved. We give him an offering twice a year, and I must say his ghost has not made trouble for us. But still am I somewhat uneasy about it.'

'Three years, eh?' breathed Whitcomb. 'I see. . . .'

It took a good hour to break away, and Wulfnoth insisted

on sending a boy along to guide them to the river. Everard, who didn't feel like walking that far, grinned and called down the hopper. As he and Whitcomb mounted it, he said gravely to the bulging-eyed lad: 'Know that thou hast guested Woden and Thunor, who will hereafter guard thy folk from harm.' Then he jumped three years back in time.

'Now comes the rough part,' he said, peering out of the thicket at the nighted thorp. The mound was not there now; the wizard Stane was still alive. 'It's easy enough to put on a magic show for a kid, but we've got to extract this character from the middle of a big, tough town where he's the king's right-hand man. *And* he has a blast-ray.'

'Apparently we succeeded – or will succeed,' said Whitcomb.

'Nope. It's not irrevocable, you know. If we fail, Wulfnoth will be telling us a different story three years from now, probably that Stane is there – he may kill us twice! And England, pulled out of the Dark Ages into a neoclassical culture, won't evolve into anything you'd recognize by 1894. ... I wonder what Stane's game is.'

He lifted the hopper and sent it through the sky towards Canterbury. A night wind whistled darkly past his face. Presently the town loomed near, and he grounded in a copse. The moon was white on the half-ruined Roman walls of ancient Durovernum, dappled black on the newer earth and wood of the Jutish repairs. Nobody would get in after sunset.

Again the hopper brought them to daytime – near noon – and was sent skywards. His breakfast, two hours ago and three years in the future, felt soggy as Everard led the way on to a crumbling Roman road and towards the city. There was a goodly traffic, mostly farmers driving creaky ox-carts of produce in to market. A pair of vicious-looking guards halted them at the gate and demanded their business. This time they were the agents of a trader on Thanet who had sent them to interview various artisans here. The hoodlums looked surly till Whitcomb slipped them a couple of Roman coins; then the spears went down and they were waved past.

The city brawled and bustled around them, though again it was the ripe smell which impressed Everard most. Among the jostling Jutes, he spotted an occasional Romano-Briton, disdainfully picking a way through the muck and pulling his shabby tunic clear of contact with these savages. It would have been funny if it weren't pathetic.

There was an extraordinarily dirty inn filling the moss-grown ruins of what had been a rich man's town house. Everard and Whitcomb found that their money was of high value here where trade was principally in kind. By standing a few rounds of drinks, they got all the information they wanted. King Hengist's hall was near the middle of town ... not really a hall, an old building which had been deplorably prettied up under the direction of that outlander Stane ... not that our good and doughty king is any panty-waist, don't get me wrong, stranger ... why, only last month ... oh, yes, Stane! He lived in the house right next to it. Strange fellow, some said he was a god ... He certainly had an eye for the girls. ... Yes, they said he was behind all this peace-talk with the Britons. More and more of those slickers coming in every day, it's getting so an honest man can't let a little blood without ... Of course, Stane is very wise, I wouldn't say anything against him, understand, after all, he can throw lightning. ...

'So what do we do?' asked Whitcomb, back in their own room. 'Go on in and arrest him?'

'No, I doubt if that's possible,' said Everard cautiously. 'I've got a sort of a plan, but it depends on guessing what he really intends. Let's see if we can't get an audience.' As he got off the straw tick which served for a bed, he was stratching. 'Damn! What this period needs isn't literacy but flea powder!'

The house had been carefully renovated, its white, porticoed façade almost painfully clean against the grubbiness around it. Two guards lounged on the stairs, snapping to alertness as the agents approached. Everard fed them money and a story about being a visitor who had news that would surely interest the great wizard. 'Tell him, "Man from tomorrow." 'Tis a password. Got it?'

'It makes not sense,' complained the guard.

'Passwords need not make sense,' said Everard with hauteur.

The Jute clanked off, shaking his head dolefully. All these newfangled notions!

'Are you sure this is wise?' asked Whitcomb. 'He'll be on the alert now, you know.'

'I also know a VIP isn't going to waste time on just any stranger. This business is urgent, man! So far, he hasn't accomplished anything permanent, not even enough to become a lasting legend. But if Hengist should make a genuine union with the Britons . . .'

The guard returned, grunted something, and led them up the stairs and across the peristyle. Beyond was the atrium, a good-sized room where modern bearskin rugs jarred with chipped marble and faded mosaics. A man stood waiting before a rude wooden couch. As they entered, he raised his hand, and Everard saw the slim barrel of a thirtieth-century blast-ray.

'Keep your hands in sight and well away from your sides,' said the man gently. 'Otherwise, I shall belike have to smite you with a thunderbolt.'

Whitcomb sucked in a sharp, dismayed breath, but Everard had been rather expecting this. Even so there was a cold knot in his stomach.

The wizard Stane was a small man, dressed in a fine embroidered tunic which must have come from some British villa. His body was lithe, his head large, with a face of rather engaging ugliness under a shock of black hair. A grin of tension bent his lips.

'Search them, Eadgar,' he ordered. 'Take out aught they may bear in their clothing.'

The Jute's frisking was clumsy, but he found the stunners and tossed them to the floor. 'Thou mayst go,' said Stane.

'Is there no danger from them, my lord?' asked the soldier.

Stane grinned wider. 'With this in my hand? Nay, go.' Eadgar shambled out. *At least we still have sword and axe,* thought Everard. *But they're not much use with that thing looking at us.*

'So you come from tomorrow,' murmured Stane. A sudden film of sweat glistened on his forehead. 'I wondered about that. Speak you the later English tongue?'

Whitcomb opened his mouth, but Everard, improvising with his life at wager, beat him to the draw. 'What tongue mean you?'

'Thus-wise.' Stane broke into an English which had a peculiar accent but was recognizable to twentieth-century ears: 'Ih want know where an' when y're from, what y'r 'tentions air, an' all else. Gimme d' facts 'r Ih'll burn y' doon.'

Everard shook his head. 'Nay,' he answered in Jutish. 'I understand you not.' Whitcomb threw him a glance and then subsided, ready to follow the American's lead. Everard's mind raced: under the brassiness of desperation, he knew that death waited for his first mistake. 'In our day we talked thus. . . .' And he reeled off a paragraph of Mexican-Spanish chatter, garbling it as much as he dared.

'So . . . a Latin tongue!' Stane's eyes glittered. The blaster shook in his hand. '*When* be you from?'

'The twentieth century after Christ, and our land hight Lyonesse. It lies across the western ocean —'

'America!' It was a gasp. 'Was it ever called America?'

'No. I wot not what you speak of.'

Stane shuddered uncontrollably. Mastering himself: 'Know you the Roman tongue?'

Everard nodded.

Stane laughed nervously. 'Then let us speak that. If you knew how sick I am of this local hog-language. . . .' His Latin was a little broken, obviously he had picked it up in this century, but fluent enough. He waved the blaster. 'Pardon my discourtesy. But I have to be careful!'

'Naturally,' said Everard. 'Ah . . . my name is Mencius, and my friend is Iuvenalis. We came from the future, as you have guessed; we are historians, and time travel has just been invented.'

'Properly speaking, I am Rozher Schtein, from the year 2987. Have you . . . heard of me?'

'Who else?' said Everard. 'We came back looking for this mysterious Stane who seemed to be one of the crucial figures of history. We suspected he might have been a time traveller, *peregrinator temporis,* that is. Now we know.'

'Three years.' Schtein began pacing feverishly, the blaster swinging in his hand; but he was too far off for a sudden leap. 'Three years I have been here. If you knew how often I have lain awake, wondering if I would succeed. . . . Tell me, is your world united?'

'The world and the planets,' said Everard. 'They have

34

been for a long time.' Inwardly, he shivered. His life hung on his ability to guess what Schtein's plans were.

'And are you a free people?'

'We are. That is to say, the Emperor presides, but the Senate makes the laws and it is elected by the people.'

There was an almost holy look on the gnomish face, transfiguring it. 'As I dreamed,' whispered Schtein. 'Thank you.'

'So you came back from your period to . . . create history?'

'No,' said Schtein. 'To change it.'

Words tumbled out of him, as if he had wished to speak and dared not for many years: 'I was a historian too. By chance I met a man who claimed to be a merchant from the Saturnian moons, but since I had lived there once, I saw through the fraud. Investigating, I learned the truth. He was a time traveller from the very far future.

'You must understand, the age I lived in was a terrible one, and as a psychographic historian I realized that the war, poverty, and tyranny which cursed us were not due to any innate evil in man, but to simple cause and effect. Machine technology had risen in a world divided against itself, and war grew to be an even larger and more destructive enterprise. There had been periods of peace, even fairly long ones; but the disease was too deep-rooted, conflict was a part of our very civilization. My family had been wiped out in a Venusian raid, I had nothing to lose. I took the time machine after . . . disposing . . . of its owner.

'The great mistake, I thought, had been made back in the Dark Ages. Rome had united a vast empire in peace, and out of peace justice can always arise. But Rome exhausted herself in the effort, and was now falling apart. The barbarians coming in were vigorous; they could do much, but they were quickly corrupted.

'But here is England. It has been isolated from the rotting fabric of Roman society. The Germanics are entering, filthy oafs but strong and willing to learn. In my history, they simply wiped out British civilization and then, being intellectually helpless, were swallowed up by the new – and evil – civilization called Western. I want to see something better happen.

'It hasn't been easy. You would be surprised how hard it is to survive in a different age until you know your way around, even if you have modern weapons and interesting gifts for the king. But I have Hengist's respect now, and increasingly more of the confidence of the Britons. I can unite the two peoples in a mutual war on the Picts. England will be one kingdom, with Saxon strength and Roman learning, powerful enough to stand off all invaders. Christianity is inevitable, of course, but I will see to it that it is the right kind of Christianity, one which will educate and civilize men without shackling their minds.

'Eventually England will be in a position to start taking over on the Continent. Finally, one world. I will stay here long enough to get the anti-Pictish union started, then vanish with a promise to return later. If I reappear at, say, fifty-year intervals for the next several centuries, I will be a legend, a god, who can make sure they stay on the right track.'

'I have read much about St Stanius,' said Everard slowly.

'And I won!' cried Schtein. 'I gave peace to the world.' Tears were on his cheeks.

Everard moved closer. Schtein pointed the blast-ray at his belly, not yet quite trusting him. Everard circled casually, and Schtein swivelled to keep him covered. But the man was too agitated by the seeming proof of his own success to remember Whitcomb. Everard threw a look over his shoulder at the Englishman.

Whitcomb hurled his axe. Everard dived for the floor. Schtein screamed, and the blast-ray sizzled. The axe had cloven his shoulder. Whitcomb sprang, getting a grip on his gun hand. Schtein howled, struggling to force the blaster around. Everard jumped up to help. There was a moment of confusion.

Then the blaster went off again, and Schtein was suddenly a dead weight in their arms. Blood drenched their coats from the hideous opening in his chest.

The two guards came running in. Everard snatched his stunner off the floor and thumbed the ratchet up to full intensity. A flung spear grazed his arm. He fired twice, and the burly forms crashed. They'd be out for hours.

Crouching a moment, Everard listened. A feminine scream sounded from the inner chambers, but no one was entering at the door. 'I guess we've carried it off,' he panted.

'Yes.' Whitcomb looked dully at the corpse sprawled before him. It seemed pathetically small.

'I didn't mean for him to die,' said Everard. 'But time is . . . tough. It was written, I suppose.'

'Better this way than a Patrol court and the exile planet,' said Whitcomb.

'Technically, at least, he was a thief and a murderer,' said Everard. 'But it was a great dream he had.'

'And we upset it.'

'History might have upset it. Probably would have. One man just isn't powerful enough, or wise enough. I think most human misery is due to well-meaning fanatics like him.'

'So we just fold our hands and take what comes.'

'Think of all your friends, up in 1947. They'd never even have existed.'

Whitcomb took off his cloak and tried to wipe the blood from his clothes.

'Let's get going,' said Everard. He trotted through the rear portal. A frightened concubine watched him with large eyes.

He had to blast the lock off an inner door. The room beyond held an Ing-model time shuttle, a few boxes with weapons and supplies, some books. Everard loaded it all into the machine except the fuel chest. That had to be left, so that up in the future he would learn of this and come back to stop the man who would be God.

'Suppose you take this to the warehouse in 1894,' he said. 'I'll ride our hopper back and meet you at the office.'

Whitcomb gave him a long stare. The man's face was drawn. Even as Everard watched him, it stiffened with resolution.

'All right, old chap,' said the Englishman. He smiled, almost wistfully, and clasped Everard's hand. 'So long. Good luck.'

Everard stared after him as he entered the great steel cylinder. That was an odd thing to say, when they'd be having tea up in 1894 in a couple of hours.

Worry nagged him as he went out of the building and mingled with the crowd. Charlie was a peculiar cuss. Well. . . .

No one interfered with him as he left the city and entered

the thicket beyond. He called the time hopper back down and, in spite of the need for haste lest someone come to see what kind of bird had landed, cracked a jug of ale. He needed it badly. Then he took a last look at Old England and jumped up to 1894.

Mainwethering and his guards were there as promised. The officer looked alarmed at the sight of one man arriving with blood clotting across his garments, but Everard gave him a reassuring report.

It took a while to wash up, change clothes, and deliver a full account to the secretary. By then, Whitcomb should have arrived in a hansom, but there was no sign of him. Mainwethering called the warehouse on the radio, and turned back with a frown. 'He hasn't come yet,' he said. 'Could something have gone wrong?'

'Hardly. Those machines are foolproof.' Everard gnawed his lip. 'I don't know what the matter is. Maybe he misunderstood and went up to 1947 instead.'

An exchange of notes revealed that Whitcomb had not reported in at that end either. Everard and Mainwethering went out for their tea. There was still no trace of Whitcomb when they got back.

'I had best inform the field agency,' said Mainwethering. 'Eh, what? They should be able to find him.'

'No. Wait.' Everard stood for a moment, thinking. The idea had been germinating in him for some time. It was dreadful.

'Have you a notion?'

'Yes. Sort of.' Everard began shucking his Victorian suit. His hands trembled. 'Get my twentieth-century clothes, will you? I may be able to find him by myself.'

'The Patrol will want a preliminary report of your idea and intentions,' reminded Mainwethering.

'To hell with the Patrol,' said Everard.

6

London, 1944. The early winter night had fallen, and a thin cold wind blew down streets which were gulfs of darkness. Somewhere came the *crump* of an explosion, and a fire was burning, great red banners flapping above the roofs.

Everard left his hopper on the pavement – nobody was out when the V-bombs were falling – and groped slowly through the murk. November seventeenth; his trained memory had called up the date for him. Mary Nelson had died this day.

He found a public phone booth on the corner and looked in the directory. There were a lot of Nelsons, but only one Mary listed for the Streatham area. That would be the mother, of course. He had to guess that the daughter would have the same first name. Nor did he know the time at which the bomb had struck, but there were ways to learn that.

Fire and thunder roared at him as he came out. He flung himself on his belly while glass whistled where he had been. November seventeenth, 1944. The younger Manse Everard, lieutenant in the United States Army Engineers, was somewhere across the Channel, near the German guns. He couldn't recall exactly where, just then, and did not stop to make the effort. It didn't matter. He knew he was going to survive *that* danger.

The new blaze was a-dance behind him as he ran for his machine. He jumped aboard and took off into the air. High above London, he saw only a vast darkness spotted with flame. *Walpurgisnacht*, and all hell let loose on earth!

He remembered Streatham well, a dreary stretch of brick inhabited by little clerks and greengrocers and mechanics, the very petite bourgeoisie who had stood up and fought the power which conquered Europe to a standstill. There had been a girl living there, back in 1943.... Eventually she married someone else.

Skimming low, he tried to find the address. A volcano erupted not far off. His mount staggered in the air, he almost lost his seat. Hurrying towards the place, he saw a house tumbled and smashed and flaming. It was only three blocks from the Nelson home. He was too late.

No! He checked the time – just 10.30 – and jumped back two hours. It was still night, but the slain house stood solid in the gloom. For a second he wanted to warn those inside. But no. All over the world, people were dying. He was not Schtein, to take history on his shoulders.

He grinned wryly, dismounted, and walked through the gate. He was not a damned Danellian either. He knocked on the door, and it opened. A middle-aged woman looked at him through the murk, and he realized it was odd to see an American in civilian clothes here.

'Excuse me,' he said. 'Do you know Miss Mary Nelson?'

'Why, yes.' Hesitation. 'She lives nearby. She's coming over soon. Are you a friend?'

Everard nodded. 'She sent me here with a message for you, Mrs . . . ah. . . .'

'Enderby.'

'Oh, yes, Mrs Enderby. I'm terribly forgetful. Look, Miss Nelson wanted me to say she's very sorry but she can't come. However, she wants you and your entire family over at 10.30.'

'All of us, sir? But the children —'

'By all means, the children too. Every one of you. She has a very special surprise arranged, something she can only show you then. All of you have to be there.'

'Well . . . all right, sir, if she says so.'

'All of you at 10.30, without fail. I'll see you then, Mrs Enderby.' Everard nodded and walked back to the street.

He had done what he could. Next was the Nelson house. He rode his hopper three blocks down, parked it in the gloom of an alley, and walked up to the house. He was guilty too now, as guilty as Schtein. He wondered what the exile planet was like.

There was no sign of the Ing shuttle, and it was too big to conceal. So Charlie hadn't arrived yet. He'd have to play by ear till then.

As he knocked on the door, he wondered what his saving of the Enderby family would mean. Those children would grow up, have children of their own; quite insignificant middle-class Englishmen, no doubt, but somewhere in the centuries to come an important man would be born or fail to be born. Of course, time was not very inflexible. Except in rare cases, the precise ancestry didn't matter, only the broad pool of human genes and human society did. Still, this might be one of those rare cases.

A young woman opened the door for him. She was a pretty little girl, not spectacular but nice looking in her trim uniform. 'Miss Nelson?'

'Yes?'

'My name is Everard. I'm a friend of Charlie Whitcomb. May I come in? I have a rather surprising bit of news for you.'

'I was about to go out,' she said apologetically.

'No, you weren't.' Wrong line; she was stiffening with indignation. 'Sorry. Please, may I explain?'

She led him into a drab and cluttered parlour. 'Won't you sit down, Mr Everard? Please don't talk too loudly. The family are all asleep. They get up early.'

Everard made himself comfortable. Mary perched on the edge of the sofa, watching him with large eyes. He wondered if Wulfnoth and Eadgar were among her ancestors. Yes . . . undoubtedly they were, after all these centuries. Maybe Schtein was too.

'Are you in the Air Force?' she asked. 'Is that how you met Charlie?'

'No. I'm in Intelligence, which is the reason for this mufti. May I ask you when you last saw him?'

'Oh, weeks ago. He's stationed in France just now. I hope this war will soon be over. So silly of them to keep on when they must know they're finished, isn't it?' She cocked her head curiously. 'But what is this news you have?'

'I'll come to it in a moment.' He began to ramble as much as he dared, talking of conditions across the Channel. It was strange to sit conversing with a ghost. And his conditioning prevented him from telling the truth. He wanted to, but when he tried his tongue froze up on him.

'. . . and what it costs to get a bottle of red-ink ordinaire —'

'Please,' she interrupted impatiently. 'Would you mind coming to the point? I do have an engagement for to-night.'

'Oh, sorry. Very sorry, I'm sure. You see, it's this way —'

A knock at the door saved him. 'Excuse me,' she murmured, and went out past the black-out curtains to open it. Everard padded after her.

She stepped back with a small shriek. *'Charlie!'*

Whitcomb pressed her to him, heedless of the blood still wet on his Jutish clothes. Everard came into the hall. The Englishman stared with a kind of horror. 'You. . . .'

He snatched for his stunner, but Everard's was already

out. 'Don't be a fool,' said the American. 'I'm your friend. I want to help you. What crazy scheme did you have, anyway?'

'I . . . keep her here . . . keep her from going to —'

'And do you think *they* haven't got means of spotting you?' Everard slipped into Temporal, the only possible language in Mary's frightened presence. 'When I left Mainwethering, he was getting damn suspicious. Unless we do this right, every unit of the Patrol is going to be alerted. The error will be rectified, probably by killing her. You'll go to exile.'

'I. . . .' Whitcomb gulped. His face was a mask of fear. 'You . . . would you let her go ahead and die?'

'No. But this has to be done more carefully.'

'We'll escape . . . find some period away from everything . . . go back to the dinosaur age, if we must.'

Mary slipped free of him. Her mouth was pulled open, ready to scream. 'Shut up!' said Everard to her. 'Your life is in danger, and we're trying to save you. If you don't trust me, trust Charlie.'

Turning back to the man, he went on in Temporal: 'Look, fellow, there isn't any place or any time you can hide in. Mary Nelson died tonight. That's history. She wasn't around in 1947. That's history. I've already got myself in Dutch: the family she was going to visit will be out of their home when the bomb hits it. If you try to run away with her, you'll be found. It's pure luck that a Patrol unit hasn't already arrived.'

Whitcomb fought for steadiness. 'Suppose I jump up to 1948 with her. How do you know she hasn't suddenly reappeared in 1948? Maybe that's history too.'

'Man, you *can't*. Try it. Go on, tell her you're going to hop her four years into the future.'

Whitcomb groaned. 'A give-away – and I'm conditioned —'

'Yeh. You have barely enough latitude to appear this way before her, but talking to her, you'll have to lie out of it because you can't help yourself. Anyway, how would you explain her? If she stays Mary Nelson, she's a deserter from the WAAF. If she takes another name, where's her birth certificate, her school record, her ration book, any of those bits

42

of paper these twentieth-century governments worship so devoutly? It's hopeless, son.'

'Then what can we do?'

'Face the Patrol and slug it out. Wait here a minute.' There was a cold calm over Everard, no time to be afraid or to wonder at his own behaviour.

Returning to the street, he located his hopper and set it to emerge five years in the future, at high noon in Piccadilly Circus. He slapped down the main switch, saw the machine vanish, and went back inside. Mary was in Whitcomb's arms, shuddering and weeping. The poor, damned babes in the woods!

'Okay.' Everard led them back to the parlour and sat down with his gun ready. 'Now we wait some more.'

It didn't take long. A hopper appeared, with two men in Patrol grey aboard. There were weapons in their hands. Everard cut them down with a low-powered stun beam. 'Help me tie 'em up, Charlie,' he said.

Mary huddled voiceless in a corner.

When the men awoke, Everard stood over them with a bleak smile. 'What are we charged with, boys?' he asked in Temporal.

'I think you know,' said one of the prisoners calmly. 'The main office had us trace you. Checking up next week, we found that you had evacuated a family scheduled to be bombed. Whitcomb's record suggested you had then come here, to help him save this woman who was supposed to die tonight. Better let us go or it will be the worse for you.'

'I have not changed history,' said Everard. 'The Danellians are still up there, aren't they?'

'Yes, of course, but —'

'How did you know the Enderby family was supposed to die?'

'Their house was struck, and they said they had only left it because —'

'Ah, but the point is they did leave it. That's written. Now it's you who want to change the past.'

'But this woman here —'

'Are you sure there wasn't a Mary Nelson, let us say, settled in London in 1850 and died of old age about 1900?'

43

The lean face grinned. 'You're trying hard, aren't you? It won't work. You can't fight the entire Patrol.'

'Can't I, though? I can leave you here to be found by the Enderbys. I've set my hopper to emerge in public at an instant known only to myself. What's that going to do to history?'

'The Patrol will take corrective measures ... as you did back in the fifth century.'

'Perhaps! I can make it a lot easier for them, though, if they'll hear my appeal. I want a Danellian.'

'*What?*'

'You heard me,' said Everard. 'If necessary, I'll mount that hopper of yours and ride a million years up. I'll point out to them personally how much simpler it'll be if they give us a break.'

*That will not be necessary.*

Everard spun around with a gasp. The stunner fell from his hand.

He could not look at the shape which blazed away before his eyes. There was a dry sobbing in his throat as he backed away.

*Your appeal has been considered,* said the soundless voice. *It was known and weighed ages before you were born. But you were still a necessary link in the chain of time. If you had failed tonight, there would not be mercy.*

*To us, it was a matter of record that one Charles and Mary Whitcomb lived in Victoria's England. It was also a matter of record that Mary Nelson died with the family she was visiting in 1944, and that Charles Whitcomb had lived a bachelor and finally been killed on active duty with the Patrol. The discrepancy was noted, and as even the smallest paradox is a dangerous weakness in the spacetime fabric, it had to be rectified by eliminating one or the other fact from ever having existed. You have decided which it will be.*

Everard knew, somewhere in his shaking brain, that the Patrolmen were suddenly free. He knew that his hopper had been ... was being ... would be snatched invisibly away the instant it materialized. He knew that history now read: WAAF Mary Nelson missing, presumed killed by bomb near the home of the Enderby family, who had all been at her house when their own was destroyed; Charles Whitcomb disappearing in 1947, presumed accidentally drowned. He knew that Mary was given the truth, conditioned against ever revealing it, and sent back with Charlie to 1850. He knew they would make their middle-class way through life, never feeling quite at home in Victoria's reign, that Charlie would often have wistful thoughts of what he had been in the Patrol ... and then turn to his wife and children and decide it had not been such a great sacrifice after all.

That much he knew, and then the Danellian was gone. As the whirling darkness in his head subsided and he looked with clearing eyes at the two Patrolmen, he did not know what his own destiny was.

'Come on,' said the first man. 'Let's get out of here before somebody wakes up. We'll give you a lift back to your year. 1954, isn't it?'

'And then what?' asked Everard.

The Patrolman shrugged. Under his casual manner lay the shock which had seized him in the Danellian's presence. 'Report to your sector chief. You've shown yourself obviously unfit for steady work.'

'So ... just cashiered, huh?'

'You needn't be so dramatic. Did you think this case was the only one of its kind in a million years of Patrol work? There's a regular procedure for it.

'You'll want more training, of course. Your type of personality goes best with Unattached status – any age, any place, wherever and whenever you may be needed. I think you'll like it.'

Everard climbed weakly aboard the hopper. And when he got off again, a decade had passed.

# BRAVE TO BE A KING

I

ON AN EVENING in mid-twentieth century New York, Manse Everard had changed into a threadbare lounging outfit and was mixing himself a drink. The doorbell interrupted. He swore at it. A tiring several days lay behind him and he wanted no other company than the lost narratives of Dr Watson.

Well, maybe this character could be got rid of. He slippered across his apartment and opened the door, his expression mutinous. 'Hello,' he said coldly.

And then, all at once, it was as if he were aboard some early spaceship which had just entered free fall; he stood weightless and helpless in a blaze of stars.

'Oh,' he said. 'I didn't know. . . . Come in.'

Cynthia Denison paused a moment, looking past him to the bar. He had hung two crossed spears and a horse-plumed helmet from the Achaean Bronze Age over it. They were dark and shining and incredibly beautiful. She tried to speak with steadiness, but failed. 'Could I have a drink, Manse? Right away?'

'Of course.' He clamped his mouth shut and helped her off with her coat. She closed the door and sat down on a Swedish modern couch as clean and functional as the Homeric weapons. Her hands fumbled with her purse, getting out cigarettes. For a time she did not look at him, nor he at her.

'Do you still drink Irish on the rocks?' he asked. His words seemed to come from far away, and his body was awkward among bottles and glasses, forgetting how the Time Patrol had trained it.

'Yes,' she said. 'So you do remember.' Her lighter snapped, unexpectedly loud in the room.

'It's been just a few months,' he said, for lack of other phrases.

'Entropic time. Regular, untampered-with, twenty-four

46

hours-to-the-day time.' She blew a cloud of smoke and stared at it. 'Not much more than that for me. I've been in now almost continuously since my, my wedding. Just eight and a half months of my personal, biological, lifeline time since Keith and I. . . . But how long has it been for you, Manse? How many years have you rung up, in how many different epochs, since you were Keith's best man?'

She had always had a rather high and thin voice. It was the only flaw he had ever found in her, unless you counted her being so small — barely five feet. So she could never put much expression into her tones. But he could hear that she was staving off a scream.

He gave her a drink. 'Down the hatch,' he said. 'All of it.' She obeyed, strangled a little. He got her a refill and completed his own Scotch and soda. Then he drew up a chair and took pipe and tobacco from the depths of his moth-eaten smoking jacket. His hands still shook, but so faintly he didn't think she would notice. It had been wise of her not to blurt whatever news she carried; they both needed a chance to get back their control.

Now he even dared to look straight at her. She hadn't changed. Her figure was almost perfect in a delicate way, as the black dress emphasized. Sunlight-coloured hair fell to her shoulders; the eyes were blue and enormous, under arched brows, in a tip-tilted face with the lips always just a little parted. She hadn't enough make-up for him to tell for sure if she had cried lately. But she looked very near to it.

Everard became busy filling his pipe. 'Okay, Cyn,' he said. 'Want to tell me?'

She shivered. Finally she got out: 'Keith. He's disappeared.'

'Huh?' Everard sat up straight. 'On a mission?'

'Yes. Where else? Ancient Iran. He went back there and never returned. That was a week ago.' She set her glass down on the couch arm and twisted her fingers together. 'The Patrol searched, of course. I just heard the results today. They can't find him. They can't even find out what happened to him.'

'Judas,' whispered Everard.

'Keith always . . . always thought of you as his best friend,' she said frantically. 'You wouldn't believe how often he

47

spoke of you. Honestly, Manse, I know we've neglected you, but you never seemed to be in and . . .'

'Of course,' he said. 'How childish do you think I am? I was busy. And after all, you two were newly married.'

*After I introduced you, that night beneath Mauna Loa and the moon. The Time Patrol doesn't bother with snobbishness. A youngster like Cynthia Cunningham, a mere clerk fresh out of the Academy and Attached to her own century, is quite free to see a ranking veteran . . . like myself, for instance . . . as often as they both wish, off duty. There is no reason why he should not use his skill at disguise to take her waltzing in Strauss's Vienna or to the theatre in Shakespeare's London – as well as exploring funny little bars in Tom Lehrer's New York or playing tag in the sun and surf of Hawaii a thousand years before the canoe men arrived. And a fellow member of the Patrol is equally free to join them both. And later to marry her. Sure.*

Everard got his pipe going. When his face was screened with smoke, he said: 'Begin at the beginning. I've been out of touch with you for – two or three years of my own lifeline time – so I'm not certain precisely what Keith was working on.'

'That long?' she asked wonderingly. 'You never even spent your furloughs in this decade? We did want you to come visit us.'

'Quit apologizing,' he snapped. 'I could have dropped in if I'd wished.' The elfin face looked as if he had slapped it. He backed up, appalled. 'I'm sorry. Naturally I wanted to. But as I said . . . we Unattached agents are so damned busy, hopping around in all space-time like fleas on a griddle. . . . Oh, hell,' he tried to smile, 'you know me, Cyn, tactless, but it doesn't mean anything. I originated a chimaera legend all by myself, back in Classic Greece. I was known as the *dilaiopod,* a curious monster with two left feet, both in its mouth.

She returned a dutiful quirk of lips and picked up her cigarette from the ashtray. 'I'm still just a clerk in Engineering Studies,' she said. 'But it puts me in close contact with all the other offices in this entire milieu, including headquarters. So I know exactly what's been done about Keith . . . and it isn't enough! They're just abandoning him! Manse, if you won't help him Keith is dead!'

48

She stopped, shakily. To give them both a little more time, Everard reviewed the career of Keith Denison.

Born Cambridge, Mass., 1927, to a moderately wealthy family. Ph.D. in archaeology with a distinguished thesis at the age of twenty-three, after having also taken a collegiate boxing championship and crossed the Atlantic in a thirty-foot ketch. Drafted in 1950, served in Korea with a bravery which would have earned him some fame in a more popular war. Yet you had to know him quite a while before you learned any of this. He spoke, with a gift of dry humour, about impersonal things, until there was work to be done. Then, without needless fuss, he did it. *Sure,* thought Everard, *the best man got the girl. Keith could've made Unattached easily, if he'd cared to. But he had roots here that I didn't. More stable, I guess.*

Discharged and at loose ends in 1952, Denison was contacted by a Patrol agent and recruited. He had accepted the fact of time travel more readily than most. His mind was supple and, after all, he was an archaeologist. Once trained, he found a happy coincidence of his own interests and the needs of the Patrol: he became a Specialist, East Indo-European Protohistory, and in many ways a more important man than Everard.

For the Unattached officer might rove up and down the time lanes, rescuing the distressed and arresting the law-breaker and keeping the fabric of human destiny secure. But how could he tell what he was doing without a record? Ages before the first hieroglyphics there had been wars and wanderings, discoveries and achievements, whose consequences reached through all the continuum. The Patrol had to know them. Charting their course was a job for the Specialist ratings.

*Besides all of which, Keith was a friend of mine.*

Everard took the pipe from his mouth. 'Okay, Cynthia,' he said. 'Tell me what did happen.'

2

The little voice was almost dry now, so rigidly had she harnessed herself. 'He was tracing the migrations of the different Aryan clans. They're very obscure, you know. You have to start at a point when the history is known for certain, and work backward. So on this last job, Keith was going to Iran in the year 558 BC. That was near the close of the Median period, he said. He'd make inquiries among the people, learn their own traditions, and then afterwards check back at a still earlier point, and so on. . . . But you must know all about this, Manse. You helped him once, before we met. He often spoke about that.'

'Oh, I just went along in case of trouble,' shrugged Everard. 'He was studying the prehistoric trek of a certain band from the Don over the Hindu Kush. We told their chief we were passing hunters, claimed hospitality and accompanied the wagon train for a few weeks. It was fun.'

He remembered steppes and enormous skies, a windy gallop after antelope and a feast by campfires and a certain girl whose hair had held the bittersweet of woodsmoke. For a while he wished he could have lived and died as one of those tribesmen.

'Keith went back alone this time,' continued Cynthia. 'They're always so shorthanded in his branch, in the entire Patrol, I suppose. So many thousands of years to watch and so few man-lifetimes to do it with. He'd gone alone before. I was always afraid to let him, but he said . . . dressed as a wandering shepherd with nothing worth stealing . . . he'd be safer in the Iranian highlands than crossing Broadway. Only this time he wasn't!'

'I take it, then,' said Everard quickly, 'he left – a week ago, did you say? – intending to get his information, report it to the clearing house of his speciality, and come back to the same day here as he'd left you.' *Because only a blind buckethead would let more of your lifespan pass without being there himself.* 'But he didn't.'

'Yes.' She lit another cigarette from the butt of the first. 'I got worried right away. I asked the boss about it. He obliged me by querying himself a week ahead – today – and got the answer that Keith had not returned. The information clearing house said he never came to them. So we checked with Records in milieu headquarters. Their answer was . . . was . . . Keith never did come back and no trace of him was ever found.'

Everard nodded with great care. 'Then, of course, the search was ordered which MHQ has a record of.'

Mutable time made for a lot of paradoxes, he reflected for the thousandth occasion.

In the case of a missing man, you were not required to search for him just because a record somewhere said you had done so. But how else would you stand a chance of finding him? You *might* possibly go back and thereby change events so that you did find him after all – in which case the report you filed would 'always' have recorded your success, and you alone would know the 'former' truth.

It could get very messed up. No wonder the Patrol was fussy, even about small changes which would not affect the main pattern.

'Our office notified the boys in the Old Iranian milieu, who sent a party to investigate the spot,' foretold Everard. 'They only knew the approximate site at which Keith had intended to materialize, didn't they? I mean, since he couldn't know exactly where he'd be able to hide the scooter, he didn't file precise coordinates.' Cynthia nodded. 'But what I don't understand is, why didn't they find the machine afterwards? Whatever happened to Keith, the scooter would still be somewhere around, in some cave or whatever. The Patrol has detectors. They should have been able to track down the scooter, at least, and then work backwards from it to locate Keith.'

She drew on her cigarette with a violence that caved in her cheeks. 'They tried,' she said. 'But I'm told it's a wild, rugged country, hard to search. Nothing turned up. They couldn't find a trace. They might have, if they'd looked very, very hard – made a mile-by-mile, hour-by-hour search. But they didn't dare. You see, that particular milieu is critical. Mr Gordon showed me the analysis. I couldn't follow all those symbols, but he said it was a very dangerous century to tamper with.'

Everard closed one large hand on the bowl of his pipe. Its warmth was somehow comforting. Critical eras gave him the willies.

'I see,' he said. 'They couldn't search as thoroughly as they wanted, because it might disturb too many of the local yokels, which might make them act differently when the big crisis came. Uh-huh. But how about making inquiries in disguise, among the people?'

'Several Patrol experts did. They tried that for weeks, Persian time. And the natives never even gave them a hint. Those tribes are so wild and suspicious ... maybe they feared our agents were spies from the Median king, I understand they didn't like his rule. .... No. The Patrol couldn't find a trace. And anyhow, there's no reason to think the pattern was affected. They believe Keith was murdered and his scooter vanished somehow. And what difference —'

Cynthia sprang to her feet. Suddenly she yelled – 'What difference does one more skeleton in one more gully make?'

Everard rose too, she came into his arms and he let her have it out. For himself, he had never thought it would be this bad. He had stopped remembering her, except maybe ten times a day, but now she came to him and the forgetting would have to be done all over again.

'Can't they go back locally?' she pleaded. 'Can't somebody hop back a week from now, just to tell him not to go, is that so much to ask? What kind of monsters made that law against it?'

'Ordinary men did,' said Everard. 'If we once started doubling back to tinker with our personal pasts, we'd soon get so tangled up that none of us would exist.'

'But in a million years or more – there must be exceptions!'

Everard didn't answer. He knew that there were. He knew also that Keith Denison's case wouldn't be one of them. The Patrol was not staffed by saints, but its people dared not corrupt their own law for their own ends. You took your losses like any other corps, and raised a glass to the memory of your dead, and you did not travel back to look upon them again while they had lived.

Presently Cynthia left him, returned to her drink and tossed it down. The yellow locks swirled past her face as she did. 'I'm sorry,' she said. She got out a handkerchief and wiped her eyes. 'I didn't mean to bawl.'

'It's okay.'

She stared at the floor. 'You could try to help Keith. The regular agents have given up, but you could try.'

It was an appeal from which he had no recourse. 'I could,' he told her. 'I might not succeed. The existing records show that, if I tried, I failed. And any alteration of space-time is frowned on, even a trivial one like this.'

'It isn't trivial to Keith,' she said.

'You know, Cyn,' he murmured, 'you're one of the few women that ever lived who'd have phrased it that way. Most would have said, It isn't trivial to me.'

Her eyes captured his, and for a moment she stood very quiet. Then, whispering:

'I'm sorry, Manse. I didn't realize. . . . I thought, what with all the time that's gone past for you, you would have —'

'What are you talking about?' he defended himself.

'Can't the Patrol psychs do anything for you?' she asked. Her head drooped again. 'I mean, if they can condition us so we just simply can't tell anyone unauthorized that time travel exists . . . I should think it would also be possible to, to condition a person out of —'

'Skip it,' said Everard roughly.

He gnawed his pipestem a while. 'Okay,' he said at last. 'I've an idea or two of my own that may not have been tried. If Keith can be rescued in any way, you'll get him back before tomorrow noon.'

'Could you time-hop me up to that moment, Manse?' She was beginning to tremble.

'I could,' he said, 'but I won't. One way or another, you'll need to be rested tomorrow. I'll take you home now and see that you swallow a sleeping pill. And then I'll come back here and think about the situation.' He twisted his mouth into a sort of grin. 'Cut out that shimmy, huh? I told you I had to think.'

'Manse. . . .' Her hands closed about his.

He knew a sudden hope for which he cursed himself.

3

In the fall of the year 542 BC, a solitary man came down out of the mountains and into the valley of the Kur. He rode a handsome chestnut gelding, bigger even than most cavalry horses, which might elsewhere have been an invitation to bandits; but the Great King had given so much law to his dominions that it was said a virgin with a sack of gold could walk unmolested across all Persia. It was one reason Manse Everard had chosen to hop to this date, sixteen years after Keith Denison's destination.

Another motive was to arrive long after any excitement which the time traveller had conceivably produced in 558 had died away. Whatever the truth about Keith's fate, it might be more approachable from the rear; at least, straightforward methods had failed.

Finally, according to the Archaemenid Milieu office, autumn 542 happened to be the first season of relative tranquillity since the disappearance. The years 558–553 had been tense ones when the Persian king of Anshan, Kuru-sh (he whom the future knew as Kaikhosru and Cyrus), was more and more at odds with his Median overlord Astyages. Then came three years when Cyrus revolted, civil war racked the empire, and the Persians finally overcame their northerly neighbours. But Cyrus was scarcely victorious before he must face counter uprisings, as well as Turanian incursions; he spent four years putting down that trouble and extending his rule eastward. This alarmed his fellow monarchs: Babylon, Egypt, Lydia, and Sparta formed a coalition to destroy him, with King Croesus of Lydia leading an invasion in 546. The Lydians were broken and annexed, but they revolted and had to be broken all over again; the troublesome Greek colonies of Ionia, Caria, and Lycia must be settled with; and while his generals did all this in the west, Cyrus himself must war in the east, forcing back the savage horsemen who would otherwise burn his cities.

Now there was a breathing spell. Cilicia would yield without a fight, seeing that Persia's other conquests were governed with a humanity and a tolerance of local custom such as the world had not known before. Cyrus would leave the eastern marches to his nobles, and devote himself to consolidating what he had won. Not until 539 would the war with Babylon be taken up again and Mesopotamia acquired. And then Cyrus would have another time of peace, until the wild men grew too strong beyond the Aral Sea and the King rode forth against them to his death.

Manse Everard entered Pasargadae as if into a springtime of hope.

Not that any actual era lends itself to such flowery metaphors. He jogged through miles where peasants bent with sickles, loading creaky unpainted oxcarts, and dust smoked off the stubble fields into his eyes. Ragged children sucked their thumbs outside windowless mud huts and stared at him. A chicken squawked back and forth on the highway until the galloping royal messenger who had alarmed it was past and the chicken dead. A squad of lancers trotting by were costumed picturesquely enough, baggy pants and scaly armour, spiked or plumed helmets, gaily striped cloaks; but they were also dusty, sweaty, and swapping foul jokes. Behind adobe walls the aristocrats possessed large houses with very beautiful gardens, but an economy like this would not support many such estates. Pasargadae was 90 per cent an Oriental town of twisted slimy streets between faceless hovels, greasy headcloths and dingy robes, screaming merchants in the bazaars, beggars displaying their sores, traders leading strings of battered camels and overloaded donkeys, dogs raiding offal heaps, tavern music like a cat in a washing machine, men who windmilled their arms and screamed curses – whatever started this yarn about the inscrutable East?

'Alms, lord. Alms, for the love of Light! Alms, and Mithras will smile upon you! . . .'

'Behold, sir! By my father's beard I swear that never was there finer work from a more skilled hand than this bridle which I offer to you, most fortunate of men, for the ridiculous sum of . . .'

'This way, master, this way, only four houses down to the finest sarai in all Persia – no, in all the world. Our pallets are stuffed with swan's down, my father serves wine fit for a Devi, my mother cooks a pilau whose fame has spread to the ends of the earth, and my sisters are three moons of delight available for a mere. . . .'

Everard ignored the childish runners who clamoured at his sides. One of them tugged his ankle, he swore and kicked and the boy grinned without shame. The man hoped to avoid staying at an inn; the Persians were cleaner than most folk in this age, but there would still be insect life.

He tried not to feel defenceless. Ordinarily a Patrolman could have an ace in the hole; say, a thirtieth-century stun pistol beneath his coat and a midget radio to call the hidden space-time antigravity scooter to him. But not when he might be frisked. Everard wore a Greek outfit: tunic and sandals and long wool cloak, sword at waist, helmet and shield hung at the horse's crupper, and that was it; only the steel was anachronistic. He could turn to no local branch office if he got into trouble, for this relatively poor and turbulent transition epoch attracted no Temporal commerce; the nearest Patrol unit was milieu HQ in Persepolis, a generation future-ward.

The streets widened as he pushed on, bazaars thinned out and houses grew larger. At last he emerged in a square enclosed by four mansions. He could see pruned trees above their outer walls. Guards, lean lightly armed youths, squatted beneath on their heels because standing at attention had not yet been invented. But they rose, nocking wary arrows, as Everard approached. He might simply have crossed the plaza, but he veered and hailed a fellow who looked like a captain.

'Greetings, sir, may the sun fall bright upon you.' The Persian which he had learned in an hour under hypno flowed readily off his tongue. 'I seek hospitality from some great man who may care to hear my poor tales of foreign travel.'

'May your days be many,' said the guard. Everard remembered that he must not offer baksheesh: these Persians of Cyrus's own clans were a proud hardy folk, hunters, herdsmen, and warriors. All spoke with the dignified politeness common to their type throughout history. 'I serve Croesus the Lydian, servant of the Great King. He will not refuse his roof to —'

'Meander from Athens,' supplied Everard. It was an alias which would explain his large bones, light complexion, and short hair. He had, though, been forced to stick a realistic Van Dyck effect on his chin. Herodotus was not the first Greek globetrotter, so an Athenian would not be inconveniently outré. At the same time, half a century before Marathon, Europeans were still uncommon enough here to excite interest.

A slave was called, who got hold of the majordomo, who sent another slave, who invited the stranger through the gate. The garden beyond was as cool and green as hoped; there was no fear that anything would be stolen from his baggage in this household; the food and drink should be good; and Croesus himself would certainly interview the guest at length. *We're playing in luck, lad,* Everard assured himself, and accepted a hot bath, fragrant oils, fresh clothing, dates and wines brought to his austerely furnished room, a couch and a pleasant view. He only missed a cigar.

Of attainable things, that is.

To be sure, if Keith had unamendably died . . .

'Hell and purple frogs,' muttered Everard. 'Cut that out, will you?'

4

After sunset it grew chilly. Lamps were lit with much ceremony, fire being sacred, and braziers were blown up. A slave prostrated himself to announce that dinner was served. Everard accompanied him down a long hall where vigorous murals showed the Sun, and the Bull of Mithras, past a couple of spearmen, and into a small chamber brightly lit, sweet with incense and lavish with carpeting. Two couches were drawn up in the Hellenic manner at a table covered with un-Hellenic dishes of silver and gold; slave waiters hovered in the background and Chinese-sounding music twanged from an inner door.

Croesus of Lydia nodded graciously. He had been handsome once, with regular features, but seemed to have aged a lot in the few years since his wealth and power were proverbial. Grizzled of beard and with long hair, he was dressed in a Grecian chlamys but wore rouge in the Persian manner. 'Rejoice, Meander of Athens,' he said in Greek, and lifted his face.

Everard kissed his cheek as indicated. It was nice of Croesus thus to imply that Meander's rank was but little inferior to his own, even if Croesus had been eating garlic. 'Rejoice, master. I thank you for your kindness.'

'This solitary meal was not to demean you,' said the ex-king. 'I only thought . . .' He hesitated. 'I have always considered myself near kin to the Greeks, and we could talk seriously —'

'My lord honours me beyond my worth.' They went through various rituals and finally got to the food. Everard spun out a prepared yarn about his travels; now and then Croesus would ask a disconcertingly sharp question, but a Patrolman soon learned how to evade that kind.

'Indeed times are changing, you are fortunate in coming at the very dawn of a new age,' said Croesus. 'Never has the world known a more glorious King than,' etc., etc., doubtless for the benefit of any retainers who doubled as royal spies. Though it happened to be true.

'The very gods have favoured our King,' went on Croesus. 'Had I known how they sheltered him – for truth, I mean, not for the mere fable which I believed it was – I should never have dared oppose myself to him. For it cannot be doubted, he is a Chosen One.'

Everard maintained his Greek character by watering the wine and wishing he had picked some less temperate nationality. 'What is that tale, my lord?' he asked. 'I knew only that the Great King was the son of Cambyses, who held this province as a vassal of Median Astyages. Is there more?'

Croesus leaned forward. In the uncertain light, his eyes held a curious bright look, a Dionysian blend of terror and enthusiasm which Everard's age had long forgotten. 'Hear, and bring the account to your countrymen,' he said. 'Astyages wed his daughter Mandane to Cambyses, for he knew that the Persians were restless under his own heavy yoke and he wished to tie their leaders to his house. But Cambyses became ill and weak. If he died and his infant son Cyrus succeeded in Anshan, there would be a troublesome regency of Persian nobles not bound to Astyages. Dreams also warned the Median king that Cyrus would be the death of his dominion.

Thereafter Astyages ordered his kinsman, the King's Eye Aurvagaush [Croesus rendered the name Harpagus, as he Hellenized all local names], to do away with the prince. Harpagus took the child despite Queen Mandane's protests; Cambyses lay too sick to help her, nor could Persia in any case revolt without preparation. But Harpagus could not bring himself to the deed. He exchanged the prince for the stillborn child of a herdsman in the mountains, whom he swore to secrecy. The dead baby was wrapped in royal clothes and left on a hillside; presently officials of the Median court were summoned to witness that it had been exposed, and buried it. Our lord Cyrus grew up as a herdsman.

'Cambyses lived for twenty years more without begetting other sons, not strong enough in his own person to avenge the first-born. But at last he was plainly dying, with no successor whom the Persians would feel obliged to obey. Again Astyages feared trouble. At this time Cyrus came forth, his identity being made known through various signs. Astyages, regretted what had gone before, welcomed him and confirmed him as Cambyses's heir.

'Cyrus remained a vassal for five years, but found the tyranny of the Medes ever more odious. Harpagus in Ecbatana had also a dreadful thing to avenge: as punishment for his disobedience in the matter of Cyrus, Astyages made Harpagus eat his own son. So Harpagus conspired with certain Median nobles. They chose Cyrus as their leader, Persia revolted, and after three years of war Cyrus made himself the master of the two peoples. Since then, of course, he has added many others. Whenever did the gods show their will more plainly?'

Everard lay quiet on the couch for a little. He heard autumn leaves rustle dryly in the garden, under a cold wind.

'This is true, and no fanciful gossip?' he asked.

'I have confirmed it often enough since I joined the Persian court. The King himself has vouched for it to me, as well as Harpagus and others who were directly concerned.'

The Lydian could not be lying if he cited his ruler's testimony: the upper-class Persians were fanatics about truthfulness. And yet Everard had heard nothing so incredible in all his Patrol career. For it was the story which Herodotus recorded – with a few modifications to be found in the *Shah Nameh* – and anybody could spot that as a typical hero myth. Essentially the same yarn had been told about Moses, Romulus, Sigurd, a hundred great men. There was no reason to believe it held any fact, no reason to doubt that Cyrus had been raised in a perfectly normal manner at his father's home, had succeeded by plain right of birth and revolted for the usual reasons.

Only, this tall tale was sworn to by eye-witnesses!

There was a mystery here. It brought Everard back to his purpose. After appropriate marvelling remarks, he led the conversation until he could say: 'I have heard rumours that sixteen years ago a stranger entered Pasargadae, clad as a poor shepherd but in truth a mage who did miracles. He may have died here. Does my gracious host know anything of it?'

He waited then, tensed. He was playing a hunch, that Keith Denison had not been murdered by some hillbilly, fallen off a cliff and broken his neck, or come to grief in any such way. Because in that case, the scooter should still have been around when the Patrol searched. They might have gridded the area too loosely to find Denison himself, but how could their detectors miss a time hopper?

So, Everard thought, something more complicated had happened. And if Keith survived at all, he would have come down here to civilization.

'Sixteen years ago?' Croesus tugged his beard. 'I was not here then. And surely in any case the land would have been full of portents, for that was when Cyrus left the mountains and took his rightful crown of Anshan. No, Meander, I know nothing of it.'

'I have been anxious to find this person,' said Everard, 'because an oracle,' etc., etc.

'You can inquire among the servants and townspeople,' suggested Croesus. 'I will ask at court on your behalf. You will stay here awhile, will you not? Perhaps the King himself will wish to see you; he is always interested in foreigners.'

The conversation broke up soon after. Croesus explained with a rather sour smile that the Persians believed in early to bed, early to rise, and he must be at the royal palace by dawn. A slave conducted Everard back to his room, where he found a good-looking girl waiting with an expectant smile. He hesitated a moment, remembering a time twenty-four hundred years hence. But – the hell with that. A man had to take whatever the gods offered him, and they were a miserly lot.

5

It was not long after sunrise when a troop reined up in the plaza and shouted for Meander the Athenian. Everard left his breakfast to go out and stare up a grey stallion into the hard, hairy hawk-face of a captain of those guards called the Immortals. The men made a backdrop of restless horses, cloaks and plumes blowing, metal jingling and leather squeaking, the young sun ablaze on polished mail.

'You are summoned by the Chiliarch,' rapped the officer. The title he actually used was Persian: commander of the guard and grand vizier of the empire.

Everard stood for a moment, weighing the situation. His muscles tightened. This was not a very cordial invitation. But he could scarcely plead a previous engagement.

'I hear and obey,' he said. 'Let me but fetch a small gift from my baggage, in token of the honour paid me.'

'The Chiliarch said you were to come at once. Here is a horse.'

An archer sentry offered cupped hands, but Everard pulled himself into the saddle without help, a trick it was useful to know in eras before stirrups were introduced. The captain nodded a harsh approval, whirled his mount, and led at a gallop off the plaza and up a wide avenue lined with sphinxes and the homes of the great. This was not as heavily trafficked as the bazaar streets, but there were enough riders, chariots, litters, and pedestrians scrambling out of the way. The Immortals stopped for no man. They roared through palace gates flung open before them. Gravel spurted under hoofs, they tore around a lawn where fountains sparkled, and clanged to a stop outside the west wing.

The palace, gaudily painted brick, stood on a wide platform with several lesser buildings. The captain himself sprang down, gestured curtly, and strode up a marble staircase. Everard followed, hemmed in by warriors who had taken the light battle axes from their saddlebows for his benefit. The party went among household slaves, robed and turbaned and flat on their faces, through a red and yellow colonnade, down a mosaic hall whose beauty Everard was in no mood to appreciate, and so past a squad of guards into a room where slender columns upheld a peacock dome and the fragrance of late-blooming roses entered through arched windows.

There the Immortals made obeisance. *What's good enough for them is good enough for you, son,* thought Everard, and kissed the Persian carpet. The man on the couch nodded. 'Rise and attend,' he said. 'Fetch a cushion for the Greek.' The soldiers took their stance by him. A Nubian bustled forth with a pillow, which he laid on the floor beneath his master's seat. Everard sat down on it, cross-legged. His mouth felt dry.

The Chiliarch, whom he remembered Croesus identifying as Harpagus, leaned forward. Against the tiger skin on the couch and the gorgeous red robe on his own gaunt frame, the Mede showed as an ageing man, his shoulder-length hair the colour of iron and his dark craggy-nosed face sunken into a mesh of wrinkles. But shrewd eyes considered the new-comer.

'Well,' he said, his Persian having the rough accent of a North Iranian, 'so you are the man from Athens. The noble Croesus spoke of your advent this morning and mentioned some inquiries you were making. Since the safety of the state may be involved, I would know just what it is you seek.' He stroked his beard with a jewel-flashing hand and smiled frostily. 'It may even be, if your search is harmless, that I can help it.'

He had been careful not to employ the usual formulas of greeting, to offer refreshment, or otherwise give Meander the quasi-sacred status of guest. This was an interrogation. 'Lord, what is it you wish to know?' asked Everard. He could well imagine, and it was a troublous anticipation.

'You sought a mage in shepherd guise, who entered Pasargadae sixteen summers ago and did miracles.' The voice was ugly with tension. 'Why is this and what more have you heard of such matters? Do not pause to invent a lie – speak!'

'Great lord,' said Everard, 'the oracle at Delphi told me I should mend my fortunes if I learned the fate of a herdsman who entered the Persian capital in, er, the third year of the first tyranny of Pisistratus. More than that I have never known. My lord is aware how dark are the oracular sayings.'

'Hm, hm.' Fear touched the lean countenance and Harpagus drew the sign of the cross, which was a Mithraic sun-symbol. Then, roughly: 'What have you discovered so far?'

'Nothing, great lord. No one could tell —'

'You lie!' snarled Harpagus. 'All Greeks are liars. Have a care, for you touch on unholy matters. Who else have you spoken to?'

Everard saw a nervous tic lift the Chiliarch's mouth. His own stomach was a cold lump in him. He had stumbled on something which Harpagus had thought safely buried, some-thing so big that the risk of a clash with Croesus, who was duty bound to protect a guest, became nothing. And the most reliable gag ever invented was a snickersnee . . . after rack and pincers had extracted precisely what the stranger knew. . . . *But what the blue hell do I know?*

'None, my lord,' he husked. 'None but the oracle, and the Sun God whose voice the oracle is, and who sent me here, has heard of this before last night.'

Harpagus sucked in a sharp breath, taken aback by the invocation. But then, almost visibly squaring his shoulders: 'We have only your word, the word of a Greek, that you were told by an oracle – that you did not spy out state secrets. Or even if the God did indeed send you here, it may as well have been to destroy you for your sins. We shall ask further about this.' He nodded at the captain. 'Take him below. In the King's name.'

The King!

It blazed upon Everard. He jumped to his feet. 'Yes, the King!' he shouted. 'The God told me ... there would be a sign ... and then I should bear his word to the Persian King!'

'Seize him!' yelled Harpagus.

The guardsmen whirled to obey. Everard sprang back, yelling for King Cyrus as loudly as he could. Let them arrest him. Word would be carried to the throne and ... Two men hemmed him against the wall, their axes raised. Others pressed behind him. Over their helmets, he saw Harpagus leap up on the couch.

'Take him out and behead him!' ordered the Mede.

'My lord,' protested the captain, 'he called upon the King.'

'To cast a spell! I know him now, the son of Zohak and agent of Ahriman! Kill him!'

'No, wait,' cried Everard, 'wait, can you not see, it is this traitor who would keep me from telling the King. ... Let go, you sod!'

A hand closed on his right arm. He had been prepared to sit a few hours in jail, till the big boss heard of the affair and bailed him out, but matters were a bit more urgent after all. He threw a left hook which ended in a squelching of nose. The guardsman staggered back. Everard plucked the axe from his hand, spun about, and parried the blow of the warrior on his left.

The Immortals attacked. Everard's axe clanged against metal, darted in and smashed a knuckle. He outreached most of these people. But he hadn't a cellophane snowball's chance in hell of standing them off. A blow whistled towards his head. He ducked behind a column; chips flew. An opening – he stiff-armed one man, hopped over the clashing mail-clad form as it fell, and got on to open floor under the dome. Harpagus scuttled up, drawing a sabre from beneath his robe; the old bastard was brave enough. Everard twirled to meet him, so that the Chiliarch was between him and the guards. Axe and sword rattled together. Everard tried to close in . . . a clinch would keep the Persians from throwing their weapons at him, but they were circling to get at his rear. Judas, this might be the end of one more Patrolman. . . .

'Halt! Fall on your faces! The King comes!'

Three times it was blared. The guardsmen froze in their tracks, stared at the gigantic scarlet-robed person who stood bellowing in the doorway, and hit the rug. Harpagus dropped his sword. Everard almost brained him; then, remembering, and hearing the hurried tramp of warriors in the hall, let go his own weapon. For a moment he and the Chiliarch panted into each other's faces.

'So . . . he got word . . . and came . . . at once,' gasped Everard.

The Mede crouched like a cat and hissed back: 'Have a care, then! I will be watching you. If you poison his mind there will be poison for you, or a dagger. . . .'

'The King! The King!' bellowed the herald.

Everard joined Harpagus on the floor.

A band of Immortals trotted into the room and made an alley to the couch. A chamberlain dashed to throw a special tapestry over it. Then Cyrus himself entered, robe billowing around long muscular strides. A few courtiers followed, leathery men privileged to bear arms in the royal presence, and a slave MC wringing his hands in their wake at not having been given time to spread a carpet or summon musicians.

The King's voice rang through the silence: 'What is this? Where is the stranger who called on me?'

Everard risked a peek. Cyrus was tall, broad of shoulder and slim of body, older-looking than Croesus's account suggested – he was forty-seven years old, Everard knew with a shudder – but kept supple by sixteen years of war and the chase. He had a narrow dark countenance with hazel eyes, a sword scar on the left cheekbone, a straight nose and full lips. His black hair, faintly grizzled, was brushed back and his beard trimmed more closely than was Persian custom. He was dressed as plainly as his status allowed.

'Where is the stranger whom the slave ran to tell me of?'

'I am he, Great King,' said Everard.

'Arise. Declare your name.'

Everard stood up and murmured: 'Hi, Keith.'

## 6

Vines rioted about a marble pergola. They almost hid the archers who ringed it. Keith Denison slumped on a bench, stared at leaf shadows dappled on to the floor, and said wryly, 'At least we can keep our talk private. The English language hasn't been invented yet.'

After a moment he continued, with a rusty accent: 'Sometimes I've thought that was the hardest thing to take about this situation, never having a minute to myself. The best I can do is throw everybody out of the room I'm in; but they stick around just beyond the door, under the windows, guarding, listening. I hope their dear loyal souls fry.'

'Privacy hasn't been invented yet either,' Everard reminded him. 'And VIPs like you never did have much, in all history.'

Denison raised a tired visage. 'I keep wanting to ask how Cynthia is,' he said, 'but of course for her it has been – will be – not so long. A week, perhaps. Did you by any chance bring some cigarettes?'

'Left 'em in the scooter,' said Everard. 'I figured I'd have trouble enough without explaining that away. I never expected to find you running this whole shebang.'

'I didn't myself.' Denison shrugged. 'It was the damnedest fantastic thing. The time paradoxes —'

'So what did happen?'

Denison rubbed his eyes and sighed. 'I got myself caught in the local gears. You know, sometimes everything that went before seems unreal to me, like a dream. Were there ever such things as Christendom, contrapuntal music, or the Bill of Rights? Not to mention all the people I knew. You yourself don't belong here, Manse, I keep expecting to wake up. . . . Well, let me think back.

'Do you know what the situation was? The Medes and the

Persians are pretty near kin, racially and culturally, but the Medes were top dog then, and they'd picked up a lot of habits from the Assyrians which didn't sit so well in the Persian viewpoint. We're ranchers and freehold farmers, mostly, and of course it isn't right that we should be vassals —' Denison blinked. 'Hey, there I go again! What do I mean, "we"? Anyhow, Persia was restless. King Astyages of Media had ordered the murder of little Prince Cyrus twenty years before, but now he regretted it, because Cyrus's father was dying and the dispute over succession could touch off a civil war.

'Well, I appeared in the mountains. I had to scout a little bit in both space and time – hopping through a few days and several miles – to find a good hiding place for my scooter. That's why the Patrol couldn't locate it afterwards ... part of the reason. You see, I did finally park it in a cave and set out on foot, but right away I came to grief. A Median army was bound through that region to discourage the Persians from making trouble. One of their scouts saw me emerge, checked my back trail – first thing I knew, I'd been seized and their officer was grilling me about what that gadget was I had in the cave. His men took me for a magician of some kind and were in considerable awe, but more afraid of showing fear than they were of me. Naturally, the word ran like a brushfire through the ranks and across the countryside. Soon all the area knew that a stranger had appeared under remarkable circumstances.

'Their general was Harpagus himself, as smart and tough-minded a devil as the world has ever seen. He thought I could be used. He ordered me to make my brazen horse perform, but I wasn't allowed to mount it. However, I did get a chance to kick it into time-drive. That's why the search party didn't find the thing. It was only a few hours in this century, then it probably went clear back to the Beginning.'

'Good work,' said Everard.

'Oh, I knew the orders forbidding that degree of anachronism.' Denison's lips twisted. 'But I also expected the Patrol to rescue me. If I'd known they wouldn't, I'm not so sure I'd have stayed a good self-sacrificing Patrolman. I might have hung on to my scooter, and played Harpagus's game till a chance came to escape on my own.'

Everard looked at him a moment, sombrely. Keith had changed, he thought: not just in age, but the years among aliens had marked him more deeply than he knew. 'If you risked altering the future,' he said, 'you risked Cynthia's existence.'

'Yes, Yes, true. I remember thinking of that ... at the time. . . . How long ago it seems!'

Denison leaned forward, elbows on knees, staring into the pergola screen. His words continued, flat. 'Harpagus spit rivets, of course. I thought for a while he was going to kill me. I was carried off, trussed up like butcher's meat. But as I told you, there were already rumours about me, which were losing nothing in repetition. Harpagus saw a still better chance. He gave me a choice, string along with him or have my throat cut. What else could I do? It wasn't even a matter of hazarding an alteration; I soon saw I was playing a role which history had *already* written.

'You see, Harpagus bribed a herdsman to support his tale, and produced me as Cyrus, son of Cambyses.'

Everard nodded, unsurprised. 'What's in it for him?' he asked.

'At the time, he only wanted to bolster the Median rule. A king in Anshan under his thumb would have to be loyal to Astyages, and thereby help keep all the Persians in line. I was rushed along, too bewildered to do more than follow his lead, still hoping minute by minute for a Patrol hopper to appear and get me out of the mess. The truth fetish of all these Iranian aristocrats helped us a lot – few of them suspected I perjured myself in swearing I was Cyrus, though I imagine Astyages quietly ignored the discrepancies. And he put Harpagus in his place by punishing him in an especially gruesome way for not having done away with Cyrus as ordered – even if Cyrus turned out to be useful now – and of course the double irony was that Harpagus really had followed orders, two decades before!

'As for me, in the course of five years I got more and more sickened by Astyages myself. Now, looking back, I see he wasn't really such a hound from hell, just a typical Oriental monarch of the ancient world, but that's kind of hard to appreciate when you're forced to watch a man being racked.

'So Harpagus, wanting revenge, engineered a revolt, and I

accepted the leadership of it which he offered me.' Denison grinned crookedly. 'After all, I was Cyrus the Great, with a destiny to play out. We had a rough time at first, the Medes clobbered us again and again, but you know, Manse, I found myself enjoying it. Not like that wretched twentieth-century business of sitting in a foxhole wondering if the enemy barrage will ever let up. Oh, war is miserable enough here, especially if you're a buck private when disease breaks out, as it always does. But when you fight, by God, you fight, with your own hands! And I even found a talent for that sort of thing. We've pulled some gorgeous stunts.' Everard watched life flow back into him; he sat up straight and said with laughter in his voice: 'Like the time the Lydian cavalry had us outnumbered. We sent our baggage camels in the van, with the infantry behind and horses last. Croesus's nags got a whiff of the camels and stampeded. For all I know, they're running yet. We mopped him up!'

He jarred to silence, stared awhile into Everard's eyes, and bit his lip. 'Sorry, I keep forgetting. Now and then I remember I was not a killer at home – after a battle, when I see the dead scattered around, and worst of all the wounded. But I couldn't help it, Manse! I've had to fight! First there was the revolt. If I hadn't played along with Harpagus, how long do you think I'd have lasted, personally? And then there's been the realm itself. I didn't ask the Lydians to invade us, or the eastern barbarians. Have you ever seen a town sacked by Turanians, Manse? It's them or us, and when *we* conquer somebody we don't march them off in chains, they keep their own lands and customs and ... For Mithras's sake, Manse, could I do anything else?'

Everard sat listening to the garden rustle under a breeze. At last: 'No. I understand. I hope it hasn't been too lonesome.'

'I got used to it,' said Denison carefully. 'Harpagus is an acquired taste, but interesting. Croesus turned out to be a very decent fellow. Kobad the Mage has some original thoughts, and he's the only man alive who dares beat me at chess. And there's the feasting, and hunting, and women....' He gave the other a defiant look. 'Yeah. What else would you have me do?'

'Nothing,' said Everard. 'Sixteen years is a long time.'

'Cassandane, my chief wife, is worth a lot of the trouble I've had. Though Cynthia – God in heaven, Manse!' Denison stood up and laid hands on Everard's shoulders. The fingers closed with bruising strength; they had held axe, bow, and bridle for a decade and a half. The King of the Persians shouted aloud:

'How are you going to get me out of here?'

## 7

Everard rose too, walked to the floor's edge and stared through lacy stonework, thumbs hooked in his belt and head lowered.

'I don't see how,' he answered.

Denison smote a fist into one palm. 'I've been afraid of that. Year by year I've grown more afraid that if the Patrol ever finds me it'll . . . You've got to help.'

'I tell you, I can't!' Everard's voice cracked. He did not turn around. 'Think it over. You must have done so already. You're not some lousy little barbarian chief whose career won't make a lot of difference a hundred years from now. You're Cyrus, the founder of the Persian Empire, a key figure in a key milieu. If Cyrus goes, so does the whole future! There won't have been any twentieth-century with Cynthia in it.'

'Are you certain?' pleaded the man at his back.

'I boned up on the facts before hopping here,' said Everard through clenched jaws. 'Stop kidding yourself. We're prejudiced against the Persians because at one time they were the enemies of Greece, and we happen to get some of the more conspicuous features of our own culture from Hellenic sources. But the Persians are at least as important!

'You've watched it happen. Sure, they're pretty brutal by your standards: the whole era is, including the Greeks. And they're not democratic, but you can't blame them for not making a European invention outside their whole mental horizon. What counts is this:

'Persia was the first conquering power which made an effort to respect and conciliate the people it took over; which obeyed its own laws; which pacified enough territory to open steady contact with the Far East; which created a viable world-religion, Zoroastrianism, not limited to any one race or locality. Maybe you don't know how much Christian belief and ritual is of Mithraic origin, but believe me, it's plenty. Not to mention Judaism, which you, Cyrus the Great, are personally going to rescue. Remember? You'll take over Babylon and allow those Jews who've kept their identity to return home; without you, they'd be swallowed up and lost in the general ruck as the ten other tribes already have been.

'Even when it gets decadent, the Persian Empire will be a matrix for civilization. What were most of Alexander's conquests but just taking over Persian territory? And that spread Hellenism through the known world! And there'll be Persian successor states: Pontus, Parthia, the Persia of Firduzi and Omar and Hafiz, the Iran we know and the Iran of a future beyond the twentieth-century. . . .'

Everard turned on his heel. 'If you quit,' he said, 'I can imagine them still building ziggurats and reading entrails – and running through the woods up in Europe, with America undiscovered – three thousand years from now!'

Denison sagged. 'Yeah,' he answered. 'I thought so.'

He paced awhile, hands behind his back. The dark face looked older each minute. 'Thirteen more years,' he murmured, almost to himself. 'In thirteen years I'll fall in battle against the nomads. I don't know exactly how. One way or another, circumstances will force me to it. Why not? They've forced me into everything else I've done, willy-nilly . . . in spite of everything I can do to train him, I know my own son Cambyses will turn out to be a sadistic incompetent and it will take Darius to save the empire – God!' He covered his face with a flowing sleeve. 'Excuse me. I do despise self-pity, but I can't help this.'

Everard sat down, avoiding the sight. He heard how the breath rattled in Denison's lungs.

Finally the King poured wine into two chalices, joined Everard on the bench and said in a dry tone: 'Sorry. I'm okay now. And I haven't given up yet.'

'I can refer your problem to headquarters,' said Everard with a touch of sarcasm.

Denison echoed it: 'Thanks, little chum. I remember their attitude well enough. We're expendable. They'll interdict the entire lifetime of Cyrus to visitors, just so I won't be tempted, and send me a nice message. They will point out that I'm the absolute monarch of a civilized people, with palaces, slaves, vintages, chefs, entertainers, concubines, and hunting grounds at my disposal in unlimited quantities, so what am I complaining about? No, Manse, this is something you and I will have to work out between us.'

Everard clenched his fists till he felt the nails bite into the palms. 'You're putting me in a hell of a spot, Keith,' he said.

'I'm only asking you to think on the problem – and Ahriman damn you, you will!' Again the fingers closed on his flesh, and the conqueror of the East snapped forth a command. The old Keith would never have taken that tone, thought Everard, anger flickering up; and he thought:

*If you don't come home, and Cynthia is told that you never will. ... She could come back and join you, one more foreign girl in the King's harem won't affect history. But if I reported to headquarters before seeing her, reported the problem as insoluble, which it doubtless is in fact ... why, then the reign of Cyrus would be interdicted and she could not join you.*

'I've been over this ground before, with myself,' said Denison more calmly. 'I know the implications as well as you do. But look, I can show you the cave where my machine rested for those few hours. You could go back to the moment I appeared there and warn me.'

'No,' said Everard. 'That's out. Two reasons. First, the regulation against that sort of thing, which is a sensible one. They might make an exception under different circumstances, but there's a second reason too: you are Cyrus. They're not going to wipe out an entire future for one man's sake.'

*Would I do it for one woman's? I'm not sure. I hope not. ... Cynthia wouldn't have to know the facts. It would be kinder if she didn't. I could use my Unattached authority to keep the truth secret from lower echelons and tell her nothing except that Keith had irrevocably died under circumstances which forced us to shut off this period to time traffic. She'd grieve awhile, of course, but she's too healthy to mourn for ever. ... Sure, it's a lousy trick. But wouldn't it be kinder in the long run than letting her come back here, to servile status, and share her man with at least the dozen princesses that politics forces him to be married to? Wouldn't it be better for her to make a clean break and a fresh start, among her own people?*

'Uh-huh,' said Denison. 'I mentioned that idea only to dispose of it. But there must be some other way. Look, Manse, sixteen years ago a situation existed from which everything else has followed, not through human caprice but through the sheer logic of events. Suppose I had not showed up? Mightn't Harpagus have found a different pseudo-Cyrus? The exact identity of the King doesn't matter. Another Cyrus would have acted differently from me in a million day-to-day details. Naturally. But if he wasn't a hopeless moron or maniac, if he was a reasonably able and decent person – give me credit for being that much – then his career would have been the same as mine in all the important ways, the ways that got into the history books. You know that as well as I do. Except at the crucial points, time always reverts to its own shape. The small differences damp out in days or years, negative feedback. It's only at key instants that a positive feedback can be set up and the effects multiply with passing time instead of disappearing. You know that!'

'Sure,' said Everard. 'But judging from your own account, your appearance in the cave *was* crucial. It was that which put the idea in Harpagus's head. Without it, well, I can imagine a decadent Median Empire falling apart, maybe falling prey to Lydia, or to the Turanians, because the Persians wouldn't have had the kind of royal divine-right-by-birth leadership they needed. . . . No. I wouldn't come near that moment in the cave without authorization from anyone less than a Danellian.'

Denison looked at him over a raised chalice, lowered it and kept on looking. His face congealed into a stranger's. He said at last, very softly:

'You don't want me to come back, do you?'

Everard leaped off the bench. He dropped his own cup, it rang on the floor and wine ran from it like blood.

'Shut up!' he yelled.

Denison nodded. 'I am the King,' he said. 'If I raise my finger, those guards will hack you in pieces.'

'That's a hell of a way to get my help,' growled Everard.

Denison's body jerked. He sat motionless for a while, before he got out: 'I'm sorry. You don't realize what a shock . . . Oh, yes, yes, it hasn't been a bad life. It's had more colour in it than most, and this business of being quasidivine grows on you. I suppose that's why I'll take the field beyond the

Jaxartes, thirteen years from now: because I can't do anything else, with all those young lion eyes on me. Hell, I may even think it was worth it.'

His expression writhed smilewards. 'Some of my girls have been absolute knockouts. And there's always Cassandane. I made her my chief wife because in a dark way she reminds me of Cynthia. I think. It's hard to tell, after all this time. The twentieth century isn't real to me. And there's more actual satisfaction in a good horse than a sports car . . . and I know my work here is valuable, which isn't a knowledge granted to many. . . . Yeh, I'm sorry I barked at you. I know you'd help if you dared. Since you don't, and I don't blame you, you needn't regret it for my sake.'

'Cut that out!' groaned Everard.

It felt as if there were gears in his brain, spinning against emptiness. Overhead he saw a painted roof, where a youth killed a bull, and the Bull was the Sun and the Man. Beyond columns and vines trod guards in dragon skin mailcoats, their bows strung, their faces like carved wood. The harem wing of the palace could be glimpsed where a hundred or a thousand young women counted themselves fortunate to await the King's occasional pleasure. Beyond the city walls lay harvest fields where peasants readied sacrifice to an Earth Mother who was old in this land when the Aryans came, and that was in a dark pre-dawn past. High over the walls floated the mountains, haunted by wolf, lion, boar, and demon. It was too alien a place. Everard had thought himself hardened to otherness, but now he wanted suddenly to run and hide, up to his own century and his own people and a forgetting.

He said in a careful voice, 'Let me consult a few associates. We can check the whole period in detail. There might be some kind of switch point where . . . I'm not competent to handle this alone, Keith. Let me go back upstairs and get some advice. If we work out anything we'll return to . . . this very night.'

'Where's your scooter?' asked Denison.

Everard waved a hand. 'Up in the hills.'

Denison stroked his beard. 'You aren't telling me more than that, eh? Well, it's wise. I'm not sure I'd trust myself, if I knew where a time machine could be got.'

'I don't mean that!' shouted Everard.

'Oh, never mind. Let's not fight about it.' Denison sighed. 'Sure, go on home and see what you can do. Want an escort?'

'Better not. It isn't necessary, is it?'

'No. We've made this area safer than Central Park.'

'That isn't saying much.' Everard held out his hand. 'Just get me back my horse. I'd hate to lose him: special Patrol animal, trained to time hop.' His gaze closed with the other man's. 'I'll return. In person. Whatever the decision is.'

'Sure, Manse,' said Denison.

They walked out together, to go through the various formalities of notifying guardsmen and gatekeepers. Denison indicated a palace bedchamber where he said he would be every night for a week, as a rendezvous. And then at last Everard kissed the King's feet, and when the royal presence had departed he got aboard his horse and jogged slowly out through the palace gates.

He felt empty inside. There was really nothing to be done; and he had promised to come back himself and pass that sentence upon the King.

8

Late that day he was in the hills, where cedars gloomed above cold, brawling brooks and the side road on to which he had turned became a rutted upward track. Though arid enough, the Iran of this age still had a few such forests. The horse plodded beneath him, worn down. He should find some herdsman's house and request lodging, simply to spare the creature. But no, there would be a full moon, he could walk if he must and reach the scooter before sunrise. He didn't think he could sleep.

A place of long sere grass and ripe berries did invite him to rest, though. He had food in the saddlebags, a wineskin, and a stomach unfilled since dawn. He clucked encouragingly to the horse and turned.

Something caught his eye. Far down the road, level sunlight glowed off a dust cloud. It grew bigger even as he watched. Several riders, he guessed, coming in one devil of a hurry. King's messengers? But why, into this section? Uneasiness tickled his nerves. He put on his helmet cap, buckled the helmet itself above, hung shield on arm and loosened the

74

short sword in its sheath. Doubtless the party would just hurrah on past him, but. . . .

Now he could see that there were eight men. They had good horseflesh beneath them, and the rearmost led a string of remounts. Nevertheless the animals were pretty jaded; sweat had made streaks down their dusty flanks and manes were plastered to necks. It must have been a long gallop. The riders were decently clad in the usual full white pants, shirt, boots, cloak, and tall brimless hat: not courtiers or professional soldiers, but not bandits either. They were armed with sabres, bows, and lariats.

Suddenly Everard recognized the greybeard at their head. It exploded in him: Harpagus!

And through whirling haze he could also see – even for ancient Iranians, the followers were a tough-looking crew.

'Oh-oh,' said Everard, half aloud. 'School's out.'

His mind clicked over. There wasn't time to be afraid, only to think. Harpagus had no other obvious motive for hightailing into the hills than to catch the Greek Meander. Surely, in a court riddled with spies and blabbermouths, Harpagus would have learned within an hour that the King spoke to the stranger as an equal in some unknown tongue and let him go back northward. It would take the Chiliarch a while longer to manufacture some excuse for leaving the palace, round up his personal bully boys, and give chase. Why? Because 'Cyrus' had once appeared in these uplands, riding some device which Harpagus had coveted. No fool, the Mede must never have been satisfied with the evasive yarn Keith had handed him. It would seem reasonable that one day another mage from the King's home country must appear; and this time Harpagus would not let the engine go from him so easily.

Everard paused no longer. They were only a hundred yards away. He could see the Chiliarch's eyes glitter beneath shaggy brows. He spurred his horse, off the road and across the meadow.

'Stop!' yelled a remembered voice behind him. 'Stop, Greek!'

Everard got an exhausted trot out of his mount. The cedars threw long shadows across him.

'Stop or we shoot! ... halt! ... shoot, then! Not to kill! Get the steed!'

At the forest edge, Everard slipped from his saddle. He heard an angry whirr and a score of thumps. The horse screamed. Everard cast a glance behind; the poor beast was on its knees. By God, somebody would pay for this! But he was one man and they were eight. He hurried under the trees. A shaft smote a trunk by his left shoulder, burying itself.

He ran, crouched, zigzag in a chilly sweet-smelling twilight. Now and then a low branch whipped across his face. He could have used more underbrush, there were some Algonquian stunts for a hunted man to try, but at least the soft floor was noiseless under his sandals. The Persians were lost to sight. Almost instinctively, they had tried to ride after him. Cracking and crashing and loud obscenities ripped the air to show how well that had worked.

They'd come on foot in a minute. He cocked his head. A faint rush of water. ... He moved in its direction, up a steep boulder-strewn slope. His hunters were not helpless urbanites, he thought. At least some of them were sure to be mountaineers, with eyes to read the dimmest signs of his passage. He had to break the trail; then he could hole up until Harpagus must return to court duties. The breath grew harsh in his throat. Behind him voices snapped forth, a note of decision, but he couldn't make out what was said. Too far. And the blood pounded so loudly in his ears.

If Harpagus had fired on the King's guest, then Harpagus surely did not intend that this guest should ever report it to the King. Capture, torture till he revealed where the machine lay and how to operate it, and a final mercy of cold steel were the programme. *Judas*, thought Everard through the clamour of his veins, *I've mucked this operation up till it's a manual of how not to be a Patrolman. And the first item is, don't think so hard about a certain girl who isn't yours that you neglect elementary precautions.*

He came out on the edge of a high, wet bank. A brook rolled valleywards below him. They'd see he had come this far, but it would be a toss-up which way he splashed in the stream bed ... which should it be, anyhow? ... the mud was cold and slippery on his skin as he scrambled down. Better go upstream. That would bring him closer to his scooter, and

Harpagus might assume it more likely he'd try to double back to the King.

Stones bruised his feet and the water numbed them. The trees made a wall above either bank, so that he was roofed by a narrow strip of sky whose blue deepened momentarily. High up there floated an eagle. The air grew colder. But he had one piece of luck; the brook twisted like a snake in delirium and he had quickly slipped and stumbled his way from sight of his entry point. *I'll go on a mile or so,* he thought, *and maybe there'll be an overhanging branch I can grab so I won't leave an outgoing trail.* Slow minutes passed.

*So I get to the scooter,* he thought, *and go upstairs and ask my chiefs for help. I know damn well they aren't going to give me any. Why not sacrifice one man to insure their own existence and everything they care about? Therefore Keith is stuck here, with thirteen years to go till the barbarians cut him down. But Cynthia will still be young in thirteen years, and after so long a nightmare of exile and knowing her man's time to die, she'd be cut off, an alien in an interdicted era, alone in the frightened court of mad Cambyses II. . . . No, I've got to keep the truth from her, keep her at home, thinking Keith is dead. He'd want it that way himself. And after a year or two she'd be happy again; I could teach her to be happy.*

He had stopped noticing how the rocks smashed at his thinly shod feet, how his body pitched and staggered or how noisy the water was. But then he came around a bend and saw the Persians.

There were two of them, wading downstream. Evidently his capture meant enough to overcome their religious prejudice against defiling a river. Two more walked above, threading the trees on either bank. One of the latter was Harpagus. Their long swords hissed from the scabbards.

'Stop!' called the Chiliarch. 'Halt, Greek! Yield!'

Everard stood death-still. The water purled about his ankles. The pair who splashed to meet him were unreal down here in a well of shadow, their dark faces blotted out so that he saw only white clothes and a shimmer along sabre blades. It hit him in the belly: the pursuers had seen his trail down into the brook. So they split up, half in each direction, running faster on solid ground than he could move in the bed. Having gone beyond his possible range, they started working their way back, more slowly when they were bound

77

to the stream's course but quite certain of their quarry.

'Take him alive,' reminded Harpagus. 'Hamstring him if you must, but take him alive.'

Everard snarled and turned towards that bank. 'Okay, buster, you asked for it,' he said in English. The two men in the water yelled and began to run. One tripped and went on his face. The man opposite tobagganed down the slope on his backside.

The mud was slippery. Everard chopped the lower edge of his shield into it and toiled up. Harpagus moved coolly to await him. As he came near, the old noble's blade whirred, striking from above. Everard rolled his head and caught the blow on his helmet, which bonged. The edge slid down a cheekpiece and cut his right shoulder, but not badly. He felt only a sting and then was too busy to feel anything.

He didn't expect to win out. But he would make them kill him, and pay for the privilege.

He came on to grass and raised his shield just in time to protect his eyes. Harpagus probed for the knees. Everard beat that aside with his own short sword. The Median sabre whistled. But at close quarters a lightly armed Asian hadn't a chance against the hoplite, as history was to prove a couple of generations hence. *By God*, thought Everard, *if only I had cuirass and greaves, I might be able to take all four of 'em!* He used his big shield with skill, put it in front of every blow and thrust, and always worked near to get beneath the longer blade and into Harpagus's defenceless guts.

The Chiliarch grinned tautly through tangled grey whiskers and skipped away. A play for time, of course. It succeeded. The other three men climbed the bank, shouted and rushed. It was a disorderly attack. Superb fighters as individuals, the Persians had never developed the mass discipline of Europe, on which they would break themselves at Marathon and Gaugamela. But four against unarmoured one was impossible odds.

Everard got his back to a tree bole. The first man came in recklessly, sword clashing on the Greek shield. Everard's blade darted from behind the bronze oblong. There was a soft, somehow heavy resistance. He knew that feeling from other days, pulling his weapon out and stepped quickly aside. The Persian sat down, spilling out his life. He groaned once, saw he was a dead man, and raised his face towards the sky.

His mates were already at Everard, one to a side. Overhanging boughs made lassos useless; they would have to do battle. The Patrolman held off the left-hand blade with his shield. That exposed his right ribs, but since his opponents were ordered not to kill he could afford it. The right-hand man slashed at Everard's ankles. Everard sprang in the air and the sword hissed under his feet. The left-hand attacker stabbed low. Everard sensed a dull shock and saw steel in his calf. He jerked free. A sunset ray came between bunched needles and touched the blood, making it an impossibly brilliant red. Everard felt that leg buckle under him.

'So, so,' cried Harpagus, hovering ten feet away. 'Chop him!'

Everard growled above his shield rim: 'A task your jackal leader has no courage to attempt for himself, after I drove him back with his tail between his legs!'

It was calculated. The attack on him stopped a bare instant. He reeled forward. 'If you Persians must be the dogs of a Mede,' he croaked, 'can you not choose a Mede who is a man, rather than this creature which betrayed its king and now runs from a single Greek?'

Even this far west and this long ago, an Oriental could not lose face in such a manner. Not that Harpagus had ever been a coward; Everard knew how unfair his taunts were. But the Chiliarch spat a curse and dashed at him. Everard had a moment's glimpse of eyes wild in a sunken hook-nosed face. He lumbered lopsidedly forward. The two Persians hesitated for a second more. That was long enough for Everard and Harpagus to meet. The Median sabre rose and fell, bounced off Greek helmet and shield, snaked sideways for another leg cut. A loose white tunic flapped before Everard's gaze. He hunched shoulders and drove his sword in.

He withdrew it with the cruel professional twist which assures a mortal wound, pivoted on his right heel, and caught a blow on his shield. For a minute he and one Persian traded fury. At the edge of an eye, he saw the other circling about to get behind him. Well, he thought in a remote way, he had killed the one man dangerous to Cynthia. . . .

'Hold! Halt!'

The call was a weak flutter in the air, less loud than the mountain stream, but the warriors stepped back and lowered their blades. Even the dying Persian took his eyes from heaven.

Harpagus struggled to sit up, in a puddle of his own blood. His skin was turned grey. 'No ... hold,' he whispered. 'Wait. There is a purpose here. Mithras would not have struck me down unless ...'

He beckoned, a somehow lordly gesture. Everard dropped his sword, limped over and knelt by Harpagus. The Mede sank back into his arms.

'You are from the King's homeland,' he rasped in the bloody beard. 'Do not deny that. But know ... Aurvagaush the son of Khshayavarsha ... is no traitor.' The thin form stiffened itself, imperious, as if ordering death to wait upon its pleasure. 'I knew there were powers – of heaven, of hell, I know not which to this day – powers behind the King's advent. I used them, I used him, not for myself, but because I had sworn loyalty to my own king, Astyages, and he needed a ... a Cyrus ... lest the realm be torn asunder. Afterwards, by his cruelty, Astyages forfeited my oath. But I was still a Mede. I saw in Cyrus the only hope – the best hope – of Media. For he has been a good king to us also – we are honoured in his domains second only to the Persians. ... Do you understand, you from the King's home?' Dim eyes rolled about, trying to see into Everard's but without enough control. 'I wanted to capture you – to force your engine and its use from you, and then to kill you ... yes ... but not for my own gain. It was for the realm's. I feared you would take the King home, as I know he has longed to go. And what would become of us? Be merciful, as you too must hope for mercy.'

'I shall,' said Everard. 'The King will remain.'

'It is well,' sighed Harpagus. 'I believe you speak the truth ... I dare not believe otherwise. ... Then I have atoned?' he asked in a thin anxious voice. 'For the murder I did at my old king's behest – that I laid a helpless infant upon the mountainside and watched him die – have I atoned, King's countryman? For it was that prince's death ... which brought the land close to ruin ... but I found another Cyrus! I saved us! Have I atoned?'

'You have,' said Everard, and wondered how much absolution it lay in his power to give.

Harpagus closed his eyes. 'Then leave me,' he said, like the fading echo of a command.

Everard laid him upon the earth and hobbled away. The two Persians knelt by their master, performing certain rites. The third man returned to his own contemplations. Everard sat down under a tree, tore a strip from his cloak and bandaged his hurts. The leg cut would need attention. Somehow he must get to the scooter. That wouldn't be fun, but he could manage it and then a Patrol doctor could repair him in a few hours with a medical science future to his home era. He'd go to some office in an obscure milieu, because there'd be too many questions in the twentieth century.

And he couldn't afford that. If his superiors knew what he planned, they would probably forbid it.

The answer had come to him not as a blinding revelation, but as a tired consciousness of knowledge which he might well have had subconsciously for a long time. He leaned back, getting his breath. The other four Persians arrived and were told what had happened. All of them ignored Everard, except for glances where terror struggled with pride and made furtive signs against evil. They lifted their dead chief and their dying companion and bore them into the forest. Darkness thickened. Somewhere an owl hooted.

## 9

The great King sat up in bed. There had been a noise beyond the curtains.

Cassandane, the Queen, stirred invisibly. One slim hand touched his face. 'What is it, sun of my heaven?' she asked.

'I do not know.' He fumbled for the sword which lay always beneath his pillow. 'Nothing.'

Her palm slipped down over his breast. 'No, it is much,' she whispered, suddenly shaken. 'Your heart goes like a war drum.'

'Stay there.' He trod out past the drapes.

Moonlight streamed from a deep-purple sky, through an arched window to the floor. It glanced almost blindingly off a bronze mirror. The air was cold upon bare skin.

A thing of dark metal, whose rider gripped two handlebars and touched tiny controls on a panel, drifted like another shadow. It landed on the carpet without a sound and the rider got off. He was a burly man in Grecian tunic and helmet. 'Keith,' he breathed.

'Manse!' Denison stepped into the moonlight. 'You came!'

'Tell me more,' snorted Everard sarcastically. 'Think anybody will hear us? I don't believe I was noticed. Materialized directly over the roof and floated slowly down on antigrav.'

'There are guards just outside the door,' said Denison, 'but they won't come in unless I strike that gong, or yell.'

'Good. Put on some clothes.'

Denison dropped his sword. He stood rigid for an instant, then it blazed from him: 'You've got a way out?'

'Maybe. Maybe.' Everard looked away from the other man, drummed fingers on his machine's control panel. 'Look, Keith,' he said at last. 'I've an idea which might or might not work. I'll need your help to carry it out. If it does work, you can go home. The front office will accept a *fait accompli* and wink at any broken regulations. But if it fails, you'll have to come back to this very night and live out your life as Cyrus. Can you do that?'

Denison shivered with more than chill. Very low: 'I think so.'

'I'm stronger than you are,' said Everard roughly, 'and I'll have the only weapons. If necessary, I'll shanghai you back here. Please don't make me.'

Denison drew a long breath. 'I won't.'

'Then let's hope the Norns co-operate. Come on, get dressed. I'll explain as we go. Kiss this year goodbye, and trust it isn't "So long" – because if my notion pans out, neither you nor anyone else will ever see it again.'

Denison, who had half turned to the garments thrown in a corner for a slave to replace before dawn, stopped. 'What?' he said.

'We're going to try rewriting history,' said Everard. 'Or maybe to restore the history which was there in the first place. I don't know. Come on, hop to it!'

'But —'

'Quick, man, quick! D'you realize I came back to the same day as I left you, that at this moment I'm crawling through the mountains with one leg stabbed open, just to save you that extra time? Get moving!'

Decision closed upon Denison. His face was in darkness, but he spoke very low and clear: 'I've got one personal good-bye to say.'

'What?'

'Cassandane. She's been my wife here for, God, for fourteen years! She's borne me three children, and nursed me through two fevers and a hundred fits of despair, and once when the Medes were at our gates she led the women of Pasargadae out to rally us and we won.... Give me five minutes, Manse.'

'All right, all right. Though it'll take more than that to send a eunuch to her room and —'

'She's here.'

Denison vanished behind the bed curtains.

Everard stood for a moment as if struck. *You expected me to come tonight,* he thought, *and you hoped I'd be able to take you back to Cynthia. So you sent for Cassandane.*

And then, when his fingertips had begun to hurt from the tightness of his grip on the sword hilt: *Oh, shut up, Everard, you smug self-righteous whelp.*

Presently Denison came back. He did not speak as he put on his clothes and mounted the rear seat on the scooter. Everard spacehopped, an instantaneous jump; the room vanished and moonlight flooded the hills far below. A cold gust searched around the men in the sky.

'Now for Ecbatana.' Everard turned on his dashlight and adjusted controls according to notes scribbled on the pilot pad.

'Ec – Oh, you mean Hagmatan? The old Median capital?' Denison sounded astonished. 'But it's only a summer residence now.'

'I mean Ecbatana thirty-six years ago,' said Everard.

'*Huh?*'

'Look, all the scientific historians in the future are convinced that the story of Cyrus's childhood as told by Herodotus and the Persians is pure fable. Well, maybe they were right all along. Maybe your experiences here have been only one of those little quirks in space-time which the Patrol tries to eliminate.'

'I see,' said Denison slowly.

'You were at Astyages's court pretty often when you were

83

his vassal, I suppose. Okay, you guide me. We want the old guy himself, preferably alone at night.'

'Sixteen years was a long time,' said Denison.

'Hm?'

'If you're going to change the past anyway, why use me at this point? Come get me when I'd been Cyrus only one year, long enough to be familiar with Ecbatana but —'

'Sorry, no. I don't dare. We're steering close enough to the wind as it is. Lord knows what a secondary loop in the world lines could lead to. Even if we got away with it, the Patrol would send us both to the exile planet for taking that kind of chance.'

'Well . . . yes. I see your point.'

'Also,' said Everard, 'you're not a suicidal type. Would you actually want the you of this instant never to have existed? Think for a minute precisely what that implies.'

He completed his settings. The man behind him shuddered. 'Mithras!' said Denison. 'You're right. Let's not talk more about it.'

'Here goes, then.' Everard threw the main switch.

He hung over a walled city on an unfamiliar plain. Though this was also a moonlit night, the city was only a black huddle to his eyes. He reached into the saddlebags. 'Here,' he said. 'Let's put on these costumes. I had the boys in the Middle Mohenjodaro office fix 'em up to my specs. Their situation is such that they often need this type of disguise for themselves.'

Air whistled darkly as the hopper slanted earthwards. Denison reached an arm past Everard to point. 'That's the palace. The royal bedchamber is over on the east side. . . .'

It was a heavier, less graceful building than its Persian successor in Pasargadae. Everard glimpsed a pair of winged bulls, white in an autumnal garden, left over from the Assyrians. He saw that the windows before him were too narrow for entrance, swore, and aimed at the nearest doorway. A pair of mounted sentries looked up, saw what was coming, and shrieked. Their horses reared, throwing them. Everard's machine splintered the door. One more miracle wasn't going to affect history, especially when such things were believed in as devoutly as vitamin pills at home, and

84

possibly with more reason. Lamps guided him down a corridor where slaves and guards squalled their terror. At the royal bedroom he drew his sword and knocked with the pommel. 'Take over, Keith,' he said. 'You know the Median version of Aryan.'

'Open, Astyages!' roared Denison. 'Open to the messengers of Ahuramazda!'

Somewhat to Everard's surprise, the man within obeyed. Astyages as was brave as most of his people. But when the king – a thickset, hard-faced person in early middle age – saw two beings, luminously robed, haloes around their heads and fountaining wings of light on their backs, seated on an iron throne in midair, he fell prostrate.

Everard heard Denison thunder in the best tent-meeting style, using a dialect he could not follow:

'O infamous vessel of iniquity, heaven's anger is upon you! Do you believe that your least thought, though it skulk in the darkness which begot it, was ever hidden from the Day's Eye? Do you believe that almighty Ahuramazda would permit a deed so foul as you plot. . . .'

Everard didn't listen. He strayed into his own thoughts: Harpagus was probably somewhere in this very city, full of his youth and unridden as yet by guilt. Now he would never bear that burden. He would never lay a child upon the mountain and lean on his spear as it cried and shivered and finally became still. He would revolt in the future, for his own reasons, and become the Chiliarch of Cyrus, but he would not die in his enemy's arms in a haunted forest; and a certain Persian, whose name Everard did not know, would also be spared a Greek sword and a slow falling into emptiness.

*Yet the memory of two men whom I killed is printed on my brain cells; there is a thin white scar on my leg; Keith Denison is forty-seven years old and has learned to think like a king.*

'. . . Know, Astyages, that this child Cyrus is favoured of heaven. And heaven is merciful: you have been warned that if you stain your soul with his innocent blood, the sin can never be washed away. Leave Cyrus to grow up in Anshan, or burn for ever with Ahriman! Mithras has spoken!'

Astyages grovelled, beating his head on the floor.

'Let's go,' said Denison in English.

Everard hopped to Persian hills, thirty-six years futureward. Moonlight fell upon cedars near a road and a stream. It was cold, and a wolf howled.

He landed the scooter, got off and began to remove his costume. Denison's bearded face came out of the mask, with strangeness written upon it. 'I wonder,' he said. His voice was nearly lost in silence under the mountains. 'I wonder if we didn't throw too much of a scare into Astyages. History does record that he gave Cyrus a three-year fight when the Persians revolted.'

'We can always go back to the outbreak of the war and provide a vision encouraging him to resist,' said Everard, struggling to be matter-of-fact; for there were ghosts around him. 'But I don't believe that'll be necessary. He'll keep hands off the prince, but when a vassal rebels, well, he'll be mad enough to discount what by then will seem like a dream. Also, his own nobles, Median vested interests, would hardly allow him to give in. But let's check up. Doesn't the King lead a procession at the winter solstice festival?'

'Yeah. Let's go. Quickly.'

And the sunlight burned around them, high above Pasargadae. They left their machine hidden and walked down on foot, two travellers among many streaming in to celebrate the Birthday of Mithras. On the way, they inquired what had happened, explaining that they had been long abroad. The answers satisfied them, even in small details which Denison's memories recorded but the chronicles hadn't mentioned.

At last they stood under a frosty-blue sky, among thousands of people, and salaamed when Cyrus the Great King rode past with his chief courtiers Kobad, Croesus, and Harpagus, and the pride and pomp and priesthood of Persia followed.

'He's younger than I was,' whispered Denison. 'He would be, I guess. And a little smaller ... different face entirely, isn't it? ... but he'll do.'

'Want to stay for the fun?' asked Everard.

Denison drew his cloak around him. The air was bitter. 'No,' he said. 'Let's go back. It's been a long time. Even if it never happened.'

'Uh-huh.' Everard seemed more grim than a victorious rescuer should be. 'It never happened.'

Keith Denison left the elevator of a building in New York. He was vaguely surprised that he had not remembered what it looked like. He couldn't even recall his apartment number, but had to check with the directory. Details, details. He tried to stop trembling.

Cynthia opened the door as he reached it. 'Keith,' she said, almost wonderingly.

He could find no other words than: 'Manse warned you about me, didn't he? He said he would.'

'Yes. It doesn't matter. I didn't realize your looks would have changed that much. But it doesn't matter. Oh, my darling!'

She drew him inside, closed the door and crept into his arms.

He looked around the place. He had forgotten how cramped it was. And he had never liked her taste in decoration, though he had yielded to her.

The habit of giving in to a woman, even of asking her opinion, was one he'd have to learn all over again. It wouldn't be easy.

She raised a wet face for his kiss. Was *that* how she looked? But he didn't remember – he didn't. After all that time, he had only remembered she was little and blonde. He had lived with her a few months; Cassandane had called him her morning star and given him three children and waited to do his will for fourteen years.

'Oh, Keith, welcome home,' said the high small voice.

*Home!* he thought. *God!*

# THE ONLY GAME IN TOWN

## I

JOHN SANDOVAL did not belong to his name. Nor did it seem right that he should stand in slacks and aloha shirt before an apartment window opening on midtwentieth-century Manhattan. Everard was used to anachronism, but the dark hooked face confronting him always seemed to want warpaint, a horse, and a gun sighted on some pale thief.

'Okay,' he said. 'The Chinese discovered America. Interesting, but why does the fact need my services?'

'I wish to hell I knew,' Sandoval answered.

His rangy form turned about on the polar-bear rug, which Bjarni Herjulfsson had once given to Everard, until he was staring outward. Towers were sharp against a clear sky; the noise of traffic was muted by height. His hands clasped and unclasped behind his back.

'I was ordered to co-opt an Unattached agent, go back with him and take whatever measures seemed indicated,' he went on after a while. 'I knew you best, so....' His voice trailed off.

'But shouldn't you get an Indian like yourself?' asked Everard. 'I'd seem rather out of place in thirteenth-century America.'

'So much the better. Make it impressive, mysterious.... It won't be too tough a job, really.'

'Of course not,' said Everard. 'Whatever the job actually is.'

He took pipe and tobacco pouch from his disreputable smoking jacket and stuffed the bowl in quick, nervous jabs. One of the hardest lessons he had had to learn, when first recruited into the Time Patrol, was that every important task does not require a vast organization. That was the characteristic twentieth-century approach; but earlier cultures, like Athenian Hellas and Kamakura Japan – and later civilizations too, here and there in history – had concentrated on the development of individual excellence. A single graduate of the Patrol Academy (equipped, to be sure, with tools and weapons of the future) could be the equivalent of a brigade.

But it was a matter of necessity as well as aesthetics. There were all too few people to watch over all too many thousands of years.

'I get the impression,' said Everard slowly, 'that this is not a simple rectification of extratemporal interference.'

'Right,' said Sandoval in a harsh voice. 'When I reported what I'd found, the Yuan milieu office made a thorough investigation. No time travellers are involved. Kublai Khan thought this up entirely by himself. He may have been inspired by Marco Polo's accounts of Venetian and Arab sea voyages, but it was legitimate history, even if Marco's book doesn't mention anything of the sort.'

'The Chinese had quite a nautical tradition of their own,' said Everard. 'Oh, it's all very natural. So how do we come in?'

He got his pipe lit and drew hard on it. Sandoval still hadn't spoken, so he asked, 'How did you happen to find this expedition? It wasn't in Navajo country, was it?'

'Hell, I'm not confined to studying my own tribe,' Sandoval answered. 'Too few Amerinds in the Patrol as it is, and it's a nuisance disguising other breeds. I've been working on Athabascan migrations generally.' Like Keith Denison, he was an ethnic Specialist, tracing the history of peoples who never wrote their own so that the Patrol could know exactly what the events were that it safeguarded.

'I was working along the eastern slope of the Cascades, near Crater Lake,' he went on. 'That's Lutuami country, but I had reason to believe an Athabascan tribe I'd lost track of had passed that way. The natives spoke of mysterious strangers coming from the north. I went to have a look, and there the expedition was, Mongols with horses. I checked their back trail and found their camp at the mouth of the Chehalis River, where a few more Mongols were helping the Chinese sailors guard the ships. I hopped back upstairs like a bat out of Los Angeles and reported.'

Everard sat down and stared at the other man. 'How thorough an investigation did get made at the Chinese end?' he said. 'Are you absolutely certain there was no extratemporal interference? It could be one of those unplanned blunders, you know, whose consequences aren't obvious for decades.'

'I thought of that too, when I got my assignment,' Sandoval nodded. 'I even went directly to Yuan milieu HQ in Khan Baligh – Cambaluc, or Peking to you. They told me they'd checked it clear back to Genghis's lifetime, and spatially as far as Indonesia. And it was all perfectly okay, like the Norse and their Vinland. It simply didn't happen to have got the same publicity. As far as the Chinese court knew, an expedition had been sent out and had never returned, and Kublai decided it wasn't worthwhile to send another. The record of it lay in the Imperial archives, but was destroyed during the Ming revolt which expelled the Mongols. Historiography forgot the incident.'

Still Everard brooded. Normally he liked his work, but there was something abnormal about this occasion.

'Obviously,' he said, 'the expedition met a disaster. We'd like to know what. But why do you need an Unattached agent to spy on them?'

Sandoval turned from the window. It crossed Everard's mind again, fleetingly, how little the Navajo belonged here. He was born in 1930, had fought in Korea and gone through college on the GI bill before the Patrol contacted him, but somehow he never quite fitted the twentieth century.

*Well, do any of us? Could any man with real roots stand knowing what will eventually happen to his own people?*

'But I'm not supposed to spy!' Sandoval exclaimed. 'When I'd reported, my orders came straight back from Danellian headquarters. No explanation, no excuses, the naked command: to arrange that disaster. To revise history myself!'

2

Anno Domini One Thousand Two Hundred Eighty:
The writ of Kublai Khan ran over degrees of latitude and longitude; he dreamed of world empire, and his court honoured any guest who brought fresh knowledge of new philosophy. A young Venetian merchant named Marco Polo had become a particular favourite. But not all peoples desired a Mongol overlord. Revolutionary secret societies germina-

ted throughout those several conquered realms lumped together as Cathay. Japan, with the Hojo family an able power behind the throne, had already repelled one invasion. Nor were the Mongols unified, save in theory. The Russian princes had become tax collectors for the Golden Horde; the Il-Khan Abaka sat in Baghdad.

Elsewhere, a shadowy Abbasid Caliphate had refuge in Cairo; Delhi was under the Slave Dynasty; Nicholas III was Pope; Guelphs and Ghibellines were ripping up Italy; Rudolf of Habsburg was German Emperor, Philip the Bold was King of France, Edward Longshanks ruled England. Contemporaries included Dante Alighieri, Joannes Duns Scotus, Roger Bacon, and Thomas the Rhymer.

And in North America, Manse Everard and John Sandoval reined their horses to stare down a long hill.

'The date I first saw them is last week,' said the Navajo. 'They've come quite a way since. At this rate, they'll be in Mexico in a couple of months, even allowing for some rugged country ahead.'

'By Mongol standards,' Everard told him, 'they're proceeding leisurely.'

He raised his binoculars. Around him, the land burned green with April. Even the highest and oldest beeches fluttered gay young leaves. Pines roared in the wind, which blew down off the mountains cold and swift and smelling of melted snow, through a sky where birds were homebound in such flocks that they could darken the sun. The peaks of the Cascade range seemed to float in the west, blue-white, distant, and holy. Eastward the foothills tumbled in clumps of forest and meadow to a valley, and so at last, beyond the horizon, to prairies thunderous under buffalo herds.

Everard focused on the expedition. It wound through the open areas, more or less following a small river. Some seventy men rode shaggy, dun-coloured, short-legged, long-headed Asian horses. They led pack animals and remounts. He identified a few native guides, as much by their awkward seat in the saddle as by their physiognomy and clothing. But the newcomers held his attention most.

'A lot of pregnant mares toting packs,' he remarked, half to himself. 'I suppose they took as many horses in the ships as they could, letting them out to exercise and graze wherever they made a stop. Now they're breeding more as they go along. That kind of pony is tough enough to survive such treatment.'

'The detachment at the ships is also raising horses,' Sandoval informed him. 'I saw that much.'

'What else do you know about this bunch?'

'No more than I've told you, which is little more than you've now seen. And that record which lay for a while in Kublai's archives. But you recall, it barely notes that four ships under the command of the Noyon Toktai and the scholar Li Tai-Tsung were dispatched to explore the islands beyond Japan.'

Everard nodded absently. No sense in sitting here and rehashing what they'd already gone over a hundred times. It was only a way of postponing action.

Sandoval cleared his throat. 'I'm still dubious about both of us going down there,' he said. 'Why don't you stay in reserve, in case they get nasty?'

'Hero complex, huh?' said Everard. 'No, we're better off together. I don't expect trouble anyhow. Not yet. Those boys are much too intelligent to antagonize anyone gratuitously. They've stayed on good terms with the Indians, haven't they? And we'll be a far more unknown quantity. . . . I wouldn't mind a drink beforehand, though.'

'Yeh. And afterwards, too!'

Each dipped in his saddlebag, took out a half-gallon canteen and hoisted it. The Scotch was pungent in Everard's throat, heartening in his veins. He clucked to his horse and both Patrolmen rode down the slope.

A whistling cut the air. They had been seen. He maintained a steady pace towards the head of the Mongol line. A pair of outriders closed in on either flank, arrows nocked to their short powerful bows, but did not interfere.

*I suppose we look harmless,* Everard thought. Like Sandoval, he wore twentieth-century outdoor clothes: hunting jacket to break the wind, hat to keep off the rain. His own outfit was a good deal less elegant than the Navajo's Abercrombie & Fitch special. They both bore daggers for show, Mauser machine pistols and thirtieth-century stun-beam projectors for business.

The troop reined in, so disciplined that it was almost like

one man halting. Everard scanned them closely as he neared. He had got a pretty complete electronic education in an hour or so before departure – language, history, technology, manners, morals – of Mongols and Chinese and even the local Indians. But he had never before seen these people close up.

They weren't spectacular: stocky, bowlegged, with thin beards and flat, broad faces that shone greased in the sunlight. They were all well equipped, wearing boots and trousers, laminated leather cuirasses with lacquer ornamentation, conical steel helmets that might have a spike or plume on top. Their weapons were curved sword, knife, lance, compound bow. One man near the head of the line bore a standard of gold-braided yak tails. They watched the Patrolmen approach, their narrow dark eyes impassive.

The chief was readily identified. He rode in the van, and a tattered silken cloak blew from his shoulders. He was rather larger and even more hard-faced than his average trooper, with a reddish beard and almost Roman nose. The Indian guide beside him gaped and huddled back; but Toktai Noyon held his place, measuring Everard with a steady carnivore look.

'Greetings,' he called, when the newcomers were in earshot. 'What spirit brings you?' He spoke the Lutuami dialect, which was later to become the Klamath language, with an atrocious accent.

Everard replied in flawless, barking Mongolian: 'Greetings to you, Toktai son of Batu. The Tengri willing, we come in peace.'

It was an effective touch. Everard glimpsed Mongols reaching for lucky charms or making signs against the evil eye. But the man mounted at Toktai's left was quick to recover a schooled self-possession. 'Ah,' he said, 'so men of the Western lands have also reached this country. We did not know that.'

Everard looked at him. He was taller than any Mongol, his skin almost white, his features and hands delicate. Though dressed much like the others, he was unarmed. He seemed older than the Noyon, perhaps fifty. Everard bowed in the saddle and switched to North Chinese: 'Honoured Li Tai-Tsung, it grieves this insignificant person to contradict your eminence, but we belong to the great realm farther south.'

93

'We have heard rumours,' said the scholar. He couldn't quite suppress excitement. 'Even this far north, tales have been borne of a rich and splendid country. We are seeking it that we may bring your Khan the greeting of the Kha Khan, Kublai son of Tuli, son of Genghis; the earth lies at his feet.'

'We know of the Kha Khan,' said Everard, 'as we know of the Caliph, the Pope, the Emperor, and all lesser monarchs.' He had to pick his way with care, not openly insulting Cathay's ruler but still subtly putting him in his place. 'Little is known in return of us, for our master does not seek the outside world, nor encourage it to seek him. Permit me to introduce my unworthy self. I am called Everard and am not, as my appearance would suggest, a Russian or Westerner. I belong to the border guardians.'

Let them figure out what that meant.

'You didn't come with much company,' snapped Toktai.

'More was not required,' said Everard in his smoothest voice.

'And you are far from home,' put in Li.

'No farther than you would be, honourable sirs, in the Kirghiz marches.'

Toktai clapped his hand to his sword hilt. His eyes were chill and wary. 'Come,' he said. 'Be welcome as ambassadors, then. Let's make camp and hear the word of your king.'

3

The sun, low above the western peaks, turned their snow-caps tarnished silver. Shadows lengthened down in the valley, the forest darkened, but the open meadow seemed to glow all the brighter. The underlying quiet made almost a sounding board for such noises as existed: rapid swirl and cluck of the river, ring of an axe, horses cropping in long grass. Woodsmoke tinged the air.

The Mongols were obviously taken aback at their visitors and this early halt. They kept wooden faces, but their eyes would stray to Everard and Sandoval and they would mutter formulas of their various religions – chiefly pagan, but some Buddhist, Moslem, or Nestorian prayers. It did not impair the efficiency with which they set up camp, posted guard, cared for the animals, prepared to cook supper. But Everard judged they were more quiet than usual. The patterns impressed on his brain by the educator called Mongols talkative and cheerful as a rule.

He sat cross-legged on a tent floor. Sandoval, Toktai, and Li completed the circle. Rugs lay under them, and a brazier kept a pot of tea hot. It was the only tent pitched, probably the only one available, taken along for use on ceremonial occasions like this. Toktai poured *kumiss* with his own hands and offered it to Everard, who slurped as loudly as etiquette demanded and passed it on. He had drunk worse things than fermented mare's milk, but was glad that everyone switched to tea after the ritual.

The Mongol chief spoke. He couldn't keep his tone smooth, as his Chinese amanuensis did. There was an instinctive bristling: what foreigner dares approach the Kha Khan's man, save on his belly? But the words remained courteous: 'Now let our guests declare the business of their king. First, would you name him for us?'

'His name may not be spoken,' said Everard. 'Of his realm you have heard only the palest rumours. You may judge his power, Noyon, by the fact that he needed only us two to come this far, and that we needed only one mount apiece.'

Toktai grinned. 'Those are handsome animals you ride, though I wonder how well they'd do on the steppes. Did it take you long to get here?'

'No more than a day, Noyon. We have means.'

Everard reached in his jacket and brought out a couple of small gift-wrapped parcels. 'Our lord bade us present the Cathayan leaders with these tokens of regard.'

While the paper was being removed, Sandoval leaned over and hissed in English: 'Dig their expressions, Manse. We goofed a bit.'

'How?'

'That flashy cellophane and stuff impresses a barbarian like Toktai. But notice Li. His civilization was doing calligraphy when the ancestors of Bonwit Teller were painting themselves blue. His opinion of our taste has just nosedived.'

Everard shrugged imperceptibly. 'Well, he's right, isn't he?'

Their colloquy had not escaped the others. Toktai gave them a hard stare, but returned to his present, a flashlight, which had to be demonstrated and exclaimed over. He was a little afraid of it at first, even mumbled a charm; then he remembered that a Mongol wasn't allowed to be afraid of anything except thunder, mastered himself, and was soon as delighted as a child. The best bet for a Confucian scholar like Li seemed to be a book, the *Family of Man* collection, whose diversity and alien pictorial technique might impress him. He was effusive in his thanks, but Everard doubted if he was overwhelmed. A Patrolman soon learned that sophistication exists at any level of technology.

Gifts must be made in return: a fine Chinese sword and a bundle of sea-otter pelts from the coast. It was quite some time before the conversation could turn back to business. Then Sandoval managed to get the other party's account first.

'Since you know so much,' Toktai began, 'you must also know that our invasion of Japan failed several years ago.'

'The will of heaven was otherwise,' said Li, with courtier blandness.

'Horse apples!' growled Toktai. 'The stupidity of men was otherwise, you mean. We were too few, too ignorant, and we'd come too far in seas too rough. And what of it? We'll return there one day.'

Everard knew rather sadly that they would, and that a storm would destroy the fleet and drown who knows how many young men. But he let Toktai continue:

'The Kha Khan realized we must learn more about the islands. Perhaps we should try to establish a base somewhere north of Hokkaido. Then, too, we have long heard rumours about lands farther west. Fishermen are blown off course now and then, and have glimpses; traders from Siberia speak of a strait and a country beyond. The Kha Khan got four ships with Chinese crews and told me to take a hundred Mongol warriors and see what I could discover.'

Everard nodded, unsurprised. The Chinese had been sailing junks for hundreds of years, some holding up to a thousand passengers. True, these craft weren't as seaworthy as they would become in later centuries under Portuguese influence, and their owners had never been much attracted by any ocean, let alone the cold northern waters. But still, there were some Chinese navigators who would have picked up tricks of the trade from stray Koreans and Formosans, if not from their own fathers. They must have a little familiarity with the Kuriles, at least.

'We followed two chains of islands, one after another,' said Toktai. 'They were bleak enough, but we could stop here and there, let the horses out, and learn something from the natives. Though the Tengri know it's hard to do that last, when you may have to interpret through six languages! We did find out that there are two mainlands, Siberia and another, which come so close together up north that a man might cross in a skin boat, or walk across the ice in winter sometimes. Finally we came to the new mainland. A big country: forests, much game and seals. Too rainy, though. Our ships seemed to want to continue, so we followed the coast, more or less.'

Everard visualized a map. If you go first along the Kuriles and then the Aleutians, you are never far from land. Fortunate to avoid the shipwreck which had been a distinct possibility, the shallow-draft junks had been able to find anchorage even at those rocky islands. Also, the current urged them along, and they were very nearly on a great-circle course. Toktai had discovered Alaska before he quite knew what had happened. Since the country grew ever more hospitable as he coasted south, he passed up Puget Sound and proceeded clear to the Chehalis River. Maybe the Indians had warned him the Columbia mouth, farther on, was dangerous – and, more recently, had helped his horsemen cross the great stream on rafts.

'We set up camp when the year was waning,' said the Mongol. 'The tribes thereabouts are backward, but friendly. They gave us all the food, women, and help we could ask for. In return, our sailors taught them some tricks of fishing and boatbuilding. We wintered there, learned some of the languages, and made trips inland. Everywhere were tales of huge forests and plains where herds of wild cattle blacken the earth. We saw enough to know the stories were true. I've never been in so rich a land.' His eyes gleamed tigerishly. 'And so few dwellers, who don't even know the use of iron.'

'Noyon,' murmured Li warningly. He nodded his head very slightly towards the Patrolmen. Toktai clamped his mouth shut.

Li turned to Everard and said, 'There were also rumours of a golden realm far to the south. We felt it our duty to investigate this, as well as explore the country in between. We had not looked for the honour of being met by your eminent selves.'

'The honour is all ours,' Everard purred. Then, putting on his gravest face: 'My lord of the Golden Empire, who may not be named, has sent us in a spirit of friendship. It would grieve him to see you meet disaster. We come to warn you.'

'What?' Toktai sat up straight. One sinewy hand snatched for the sword which, politely, he wasn't wearing. 'What in the hells is this?'

'In the hells indeed, Noyon. Pleasant though this country seems, it lies under a curse. Tell him, my brother.'

Sandoval, who had a better speaking voice, took over. His yarn had been concocted with an eye to exploiting that superstition which still lingered in the half-civilized Mongols, without generating too much Chinese scepticism. There were really two great southern kingdoms, he explained. Their own lay far away; its rival was somewhat north and east of it, with a citadel on the plains. Both states possessed immense powers, call them sorcery or subtle engineering, as you wished. The northerly empire, Badguys, considered all this territory as its own and would not tolerate a foreign expedition. Its scouts were certain to discover the Mongols before long, and would annihilate them with thunderbolts. The benevolent southern land of Goodguys could offer no protection, could only send emissaries warning the Mongols to turn home again.

'Why have the natives not spoken of these overlords?' asked Li shrewdly.

'Has every little tribesman in the jungles of Burma heard about the Kha Khan?' responded Sandoval.

'I am a stranger and ignorant,' said Li. 'Forgive me if I do not understand your talk of irresistible weapons.'

*Which is the politest way I've ever been called a liar,* thought Everard. Aloud: 'I can offer a small demonstration, if the Noyon has an animal that may be killed.'

Toktai considered. His visage might have been scarred stone, but sweat filmed it. He clapped his hands and barked orders to the guard who looked in. Thereafter they made small talk against a silence that thickened.

A warrior appeared after some endless part of an hour. He said that a couple of horsemen had lassoed a deer. Would it serve the Noyon's purpose? It would. Toktai led the way out, shouldering through a thick and buzzing swarm of men. Everard followed, wishing this weren't needful. He slipped the rifle stock on to his Mauser. 'Care to do the job?' he asked Sandoval.

'Christ, no.'

The deer, a doe, had been forced back to camp. She trembled by the river, the horsehair ropes about her neck. The sun, just touching the western peaks, turned her to bronze. There was a blind sort of gentleness in her look at Everard. He waved back the men around her and took aim. The first slug killed her, but he kept the gun chattering till her carcass was gruesome.

When he lowered his weapon, the air felt somehow rigid. He looked across all the thick bandy-legged bodies, the flat, grimly controlled faces; he could smell them with unnatural sharpness, a clean odour of sweat and horses and smoke. He felt himself as non-human as they must see him.

'That is the least of the arms used here,' he said. 'A soul so torn from the body would not find its way home.'

He turned on his heel. Sandoval followed him. Their horses had been staked out, the gear piled close by. They saddled, unspeaking, mounted and rode off into the forest.

4

The fire blazed up in a gust of wind. Sparingly laid by a woodsman, in that moment it barely brought the two out of shadow – a glimpse of brow, nose, and cheekbones, a gleam of eyes. It sank down again to red and blue sputtering above white coals, and darkness took the men.

Everard wasn't sorry! He fumbled his pipe in his hands, bit hard on it and drank smoke, but found little comfort. When he spoke, the vast soughing of trees, high up in the night, almost buried his voice, and he did not regret that either.

Nearby were their sleeping-bags, their horses, the scooter – antigravity sled cum space-time hopper – which had brought them. Otherwise the land was empty; mile upon mile, human fires like their own were as small and lonely as stars in the universe. Somewhere a wolf howled.

'I suppose,' Everard said, 'every cop feels like a bastard occasionally. You've just been an observer so far, Jack. Active assignments, such as I get, are often hard to accept.'

'Yeh.' Sandoval had been even more quiet than his friend. He had scarcely stirred since supper.

'And now this. Whatever you have to do to cancel a temporal interference, you can at least think you're restoring the original line of development.' Everard fumed on his pipe. 'Don't remind me that "original" is meaningless in this context. It's a consoling word.'

'Uh-huh.'

'But when our bosses, our dear Danellian supermen, tell *us* to interfere . . . We know Toktai's people never came back to Cathay. Why should you or I have to take a hand? If they ran into hostile Indians or something and were wiped out, I wouldn't mind. At least, no more than I mind any similar incident in that Goddamned slaughterhouse they call human history.'

'We don't have to kill them, you know. Just make them turn back. Your demonstration this afternoon may be enough.'

'Yeah. Turn back . . . and what? Probably perish at sea. They won't have an easy trip home – storm, fog, contrary currents, rocks – in those primitive ships meant mostly for rivers. And we'll have set them on that trip at precisely that time! If we didn't interfere, they'd start home later, the circumstances of the voyage would be different. . . . Why should we take the guilt?'

'They could even make it home,' murmured Sandoval.

'What?' Everard started.

'The way Toktai was talking, I'm sure he plans to go back on a horse, not on those ships. As he's guessed, Bering Strait is easy to cross; the Aleuts do it all the time. Manse, I'm afraid it isn't enough simply to spare them.'

'But they aren't going to get home! We know that!'

'Suppose they do make it.' Sandoval began to talk a bit louder and much faster. The night wind roared around his words. 'Let's play with ideas awhile. Suppose Toktai pushes on south-eastward. It's hard to see what could stop him. His men can live off the country, even the deserts, far more handily than Coronado or any of those boys. He hasn't terribly far to go before he reaches a high-grade neolithic people, the agricultural Pueblo tribes. That will encourage him all the more. He'l, be in Mexico before August. Mexico's just as dazzling now as it was – will be – in Cortez's day. And even more tempting: the Aztecs and Toltecs are still settling who's to be master, with any number of other tribes hanging around ready to help a newcomer against both. The Spanish guns made, will make, no real difference, as you'll recall if you've read Diaz. The Mongols are as superior, man for man, as any Spaniard. . . . Not that I imagine Toktai would wade right in. He'd doubtless be very polite, spend the winter, learn everything he could. Next year he'd go back north, proceed home, and report to Kublai that some of the richest, most gold-stuffed territory on earth was wide open for conquest!'

'How about the other Indians?' put in Everard. 'I'm vague on them.'

'The Mayan New Empire is at its height. A tough nut to crack, but a correspondingly rewarding one. I should think, once the Mongols got established in Mexico, there'd be no stopping them. Peru has an even higher culture at this moment, and much less organization than Pizarro faced; the Quechua-Aymar, the so-called Inca race, are still only one power down there among several.

'And then, the land! Can you visualize what a Mongol tribe would make of the Great Plains?'

'I can't see them emigrating in hordes,' said Everard. There was that about Sandoval's voice which made him uneasy and defensive. 'Too much Siberia and Alaska in the way.'

'Worse obstacles have been overcome. I don't mean they'd pour in all at once. It might take them a few centuries to start mass immigration, as it will take the Europeans. I can imagine a string of clans and tribes being established in the course of some years, all down western North America. Mexico and Yucatan get gobbled up – or, more likely, become khanates. The herding tribes move eastward as their own population grows and as new immigrants arrive. Remember, the Yuan dynasty is due to be overthrown in less than a century. That'll put additional pressure on the Mongols in Asia to go elsewhere. And Chinese will come here too, to farm and to share in the gold.'

'I should think, if you don't mind my saying so,' Everard broke in softly, 'that you of all people wouldn't want to hasten the conquest of America.'

'It'd be a different conquest,' said Sandoval. 'I don't care about the Aztecs; if you study them, you'll agree that Cortez did Mexico a favour. It'd be rough on other, more harmless tribes, too – for a while. And yet, the Mongols aren't such devils. Are they? A Western background prejudices us. We forget how much torture and massacre the Europeans were enjoying at the same time.

'The Mongols are quite a bit like the old Romans, really. Same practice of depopulating areas that resist, but respecting the rights of those who make submission. Same armed protection and competent government. Same unimaginative, uncreative national character; but the same vague awe and envy of true civilization. The *Pax Mongolica,* right now, unites a bigger area, and brings more different peoples into stimulating contact, than that piddling Roman Empire ever imagined.

'As for the Indians – remember, the Mongols are herdsmen. There won't be anything like the unsolvable conflict between hunter and farmer that made the white man destroy the Indians. The Mongol hasn't got race prejudices, either. And after a little fighting, the average Navajo, Cherokee, Seminole, Algonquin, Chippewa, Dakota, will be glad to submit and become allied. Why not? He'll get horses, sheep, textiles, metallurgy. He'll outnumber the invaders, and be on much more nearly equal terms with them than with white farmers and machine-age industry. And there'll be the Chinese, I repeat, leavening the whole mixture, teaching civilization and sharpening wits. . . .

'Good God, Manse! When Columbus gets here, he'll find his Grand Cham all right! The Sachem Khan of the strongest nation on earth!'

Sandoval stopped. Everard listened to the gallows creak of branches in the wind. He looked into the night for a long while before he said, 'It could be. Of course, we'd have to stay in this century till the crucial point was past. Our own world wouldn't exist. Wouldn't ever have existed.'

'It wasn't such a hell of a good world anyway,' said Sandoval, as if in dream.

'You might think about your ... oh ... parents. They'd never have been born either.'

'They lived in a tumbledown hogan. I saw my father crying once, because he couldn't buy shoes for us in winter. My mother died of tb.'

Everard sat unstirring. It was Sandoval who shook himself and jumped to his feet with a rattling kind of laugh. 'What have I been mumbling? It was just a yarn, Manse. Let's turn in. Shall I take first watch?'

Everard agreed, but lay long awake.

5

The scooter had jumped two days futureward and now hovered invisibly far above to the naked eye. Around it, the air was thin and sharply cold. Everard shivered as he adjusted the electronic telescope. Even at full magnification, the caravan was little more than specks toiling across green immensity. But no one else in the Western Hemisphere could have been riding horses.

He twisted in the saddle to face his companion. 'So now what?'

Sandoval's broad countenance was unreadable. 'Well, if our demonstration didn't work —'

'It sure as hell didn't! I swear they're moving south twice as fast as before. Why?'

'I'd have to know all of them a lot better than I do, as individuals, to give you a real answer, Manse. But essentially it must be that we challenged their courage. A warlike culture, nerve and hardihood its only absolute virtues ... what choice have they got but to go on? If they retreated before a mere threat, they'd never be able to live with themselves.'

'But Mongols aren't idiots! They didn't conquer everybody in sight by bull strength, but by jolly well understanding military principles better. Toktai should retreat, report to the Emperor what he saw, and organize a bigger expedition.'

'The men at the ships can do that,' Sandoval reminded. 'Now that I think about it, I see how grossly we underestimated Toktai. He must have set a date, presumably next year, for the ships to try to go home if he doesn't return. When he finds something interesting along the way, like us, he can dispatch an Indian with a letter to the base camp.'

Everard nodded. It occurred to him that he had been rushed into this job, all the way down the line, with never a pause to plan it as he should have done. Hence this botch. But how much blame must fall on the subconscious reluctance of John Sandoval? After a minute Everard said: 'They may even have smelled something fishy about us. The Mongols were always good at psychological warfare.'

'Could be. But what's our next move?'

*Swoop down from above, fire a few blasts from the forty-first-century energy gun mounted in this timecycle, and that's the end. . . . No, by God, they can send me to the exile planet before I'll do any such thing. There are decent limits.*

'We'll rig up a more impressive demonstration,' said Everard.

'And if it flops too?'

'Shut up! Give it a chance!'

'I was just wondering.' The wind harried under Sandoval's words. 'Why not cancel the expedition instead? Go back in time a couple of years and persuade Kublai Khan it isn't worth while sending explorers eastward. Then all this would never have happened.'

'You know Patrol regs forbid us to make historical changes.'

'What do you call this we're doing?'

'Something specifically ordered by supreme HQ. Perhaps to correct some interference elsewhere, elsewhen. How should I know? I'm only a step on the evolutionary ladder. They have abilities a million years hence that I can't even guess at.'

'Father knows best,' murmured Sandoval.

Everard set his jaws. 'The fact remains,' he said, 'the court of Kublai, the most powerful man on earth, is more important and crucial than anything here in America. No, you rang me in on this miserable job, and now I'll pull rank on you if I must. Our orders are to make these people give up their exploration. What happens afterwards is none of our business. So they don't make it home. We won't be the proximate cause, any more than you're a murderer if you invite a man to dinner and he has a fatal accident on the way.'

'Stop quacking and let's get to work,' rapped Sandoval.

Everard sent the scooter gliding forward. 'See that hill?' he pointed after a while. 'It's on Toktai's line of march, but I think he'll camp a few miles short of it tonight, down in that little meadow by the stream. The hill will be in his plain view, though. Let's set up shop on it.'

'And make fireworks? It'll have to be pretty fancy. Those Cathayans know about gunpowder. They even have military rockets.'

'Small ones. I know. But when I assembled my gear for this trip, I packed away some fairly versatile gadgetry, in case my first attempt failed.'

The hill bore a sparse crown of pine trees. Everard landed the scooter among them and began to unload boxes from its sizeable baggage compartments. Sandoval helped, wordless. The horses, Patrol trained, stepped calmly off the framework stalls which had borne them and started grazing along the slope.

After a while the Indian broke the silence. 'This isn't my line of work. What are you rigging?'

Everard patted the small machine he had half assembled. 'It's adapted from a weather-control system used in the Cold Centuries era upstairs. A potential distributor. It can make some of the damnedest lightning you ever saw, with thunder to match.'

'Mmm ... the great Mongol weakness.' Suddenly Sandoval grinned. 'You win. We might as well relax and enjoy this.'

'Fix us a supper, will you, while I put the gimmick together? No fire, naturally. We don't want any mundane smoke. . . . Oh, yes, I also have a mirage projector. If you'll change clothes and put on a hood or something at the appropriate moment, so you can't be recognized, I'll paint a mile-high picture of you, half as ugly as life.'

'How about a p.a. system? Navajo chiefs can be fairly alarming, if you don't know it's just a *yeibichai* or whatever.'

'Coming up!'

The day waned. It grew murky under the pines; the air was chill and pungent. At last Everard devoured a sandwich and watched through his binoculars as the Mongol vanguard checked that camp site he had predicted. Others came riding in with their day's catch of game and went to work cooking. The main body showed up at sundown, posted itself efficiently, and ate. Toktai was indeed pushing hard, using every daylight moment. As darkness closed down, Everard glimpsed outposts mounted and with strung bows. He could not keep up his own spirits, however hard he tried. He was bucking men who had shaken the earth.

Early stars glittered above snowpeaks. It was time to begin work.

'Got our horses tethered, Jack? They might panic. I'm fairly sure the Mongol horses will! Okay, here goes.' Everard flipped a main switch and squatted by the dimly lit control dials of his apparatus.

First there was the palest blue flicker between earth and sky. Then the lightnings began, tongue after forked tongue leaping, trees smashed at a blow, the mountainsides rocking under the noise. Everard threw out ball lightning, spheres of flame which whirled and curvetted, trailing sparks, shooting across to the camp and exploding above it till the sky seemed white hot.

Deafened and half blinded, he managed to project a sheet of fluorescing ionization. Like northern lights the great banners curled, bloody red and bone white, hissing under the repeated thunder cracks. Sandoval trod forth. He had stripped to his pants, daubed clay on his body in archaic patterns; his face was not veiled after all, but smeared with earth and twisted into something Everard would not have known. The machine scanned him and altered its output. That which stood forth against the aurora was taller than a mountain. It moved in a shuffling dance, from horizon to horizon and back to the sky, and it wailed and barked in a falsetto louder than thunder.

Everard crouched beneath the lurid light, his fingers stiff on the control board. He knew a primitive fear of his own; the dance woke things in him that he had forgotten.

*Judas priest! If this doesn't make them quit. . . .*

His mind returned to him. He even looked at his watch. Half an hour . . . give them another fifteen minutes, in which the display tapered off. . . . They'd surely stay in camp till dawn rather than blunder wildly out in the dark, they had that much discipline. So keep everything under wraps for several hours more, then administer the last stroke to their nerves by a single electric bolt smiting a tree right next to them. . . . Everard waved Sandoval back. The Indian sat down, panting harder than his exertions seemed to warrant.

When the noise was gone, Everard said, 'Nice show Jack.' His voice sounded tinny and strange in his ears.

'I hadn't done anything like that for years,' muttered Sandoval. He struck a match, startling noise in the quietness. The brief flame showed his lips gone thin. Then he shook out the match and only his cigarette-end glowed.

'Nobody I knew, on the reservation, took that stuff seriously,' he went on after a moment. 'A few of the older men wanted us boys to learn it to keep the custom alive, to remind us we were still a people. But mostly our idea was to pick up some change by dancing for tourists.'

There was a longer pause. Everard doused the projector completely. In the murk that followed, Sandoval's cigarette waxed and waned, a tiny red Algol.

'Tourists!' he said at last.

After more minutes: 'Tonight I was dancing for a purpose. It meant something. I never felt that way before.'

Everard was silent.

Until one of the horses, which had plunged at its halter's end during the performance and was still nervous, whinnied.

Everard looked up. Night met his eyes. 'Did you hear anything, Jack?'

The flashlight beam speared him.

For an instant he stared blindly at it. Then he sprang erect, cursing and snatching for his stun pistol. A shadow ran from behind one of the trees. It struck him in the ribs. He lurched back. The beam gun flew to his hand. He shot at random.

The flashlight swept about once more. Everard glimpsed Sandoval. The Navajo had not donned his weapons again. Unarmed, he dodged the sweep of a Mongol blade. The swordsman ran after him. Sandoval reverted to Patrol judo. He went to one knee. Clumsy afoot, the Mongol slashed, missed, and ran straight into a shoulder block to the belly. Sandoval rose with the blow. The heel of his hand jolted upward to the Mongol's chin. The helmeted head snapped back. Sandoval chopped a hand at the Adam's apple, yanked the sword from its owner's grasp, turned and parried a cut from behind.

A voice yammered above the Mongol yipping, giving orders. Everard backed away. He had knocked one attacker out with a bolt from his pistol. There were others between him and the scooter. He circled to face them. A lariat curled around his shoulders. It tightened with one expert heave. He went over. Four men piled on him. He saw half a dozen lance butts crack down on Sandoval's head, then there wasn't time for anything but fighting. Twice he got to his feet, but his stun gun was gone by now, the Mauser was plucked from its holster – the little men were pretty good at *yawara*-style combat themselves. They dragged him down and hit him with fists, boots, dagger pommels. He never quite lost consciousness, but he finally stopped caring.

## 6

Toktai struck camp before dawn. The first sun saw his troop wind between scattered copses on a broad valley floor. The land was turning flat and arid, the mountains to the right farther away, fewer snowpeaks visible and those ghostly in a pale sky.

The hardy small Mongol horses trotted ahead – plop of hoofs, squeak and jingle of harness. Looking back, Everard saw the line as a compact mass; lances rose and fell, pennants and plumes and cloaks fluttered beneath, and under that were the helmets, with a brown slit-eyed face and a grotesquely painted cuirass visible here and there. No one spoke, and he couldn't read any of those expressions.

His brain felt sandy. They had left his hands free, but lashed his ankles to the stirrups, and the cord chafed. They had also stripped him naked – sensible precaution, who knew what instruments might be sewn into his garments? – and the Mongol garb given him in exchange was ludicrously small. The seams had had to be slit before he could even get the tunic on.

The projector and the scooter lay back at the hill. Toktai would not take any risks with those things of power. He had had to roar down several of his own frightened warriors before they would even agree to bring the strange horses, with saddle and bedroll, riderless among the pack mares.

Hoofs thudded rapidly. One of the bowmen flanking Everard grunted and moved his pony a little aside. Li Tai-Tsung rode close.

The Patrolman gave him a dull stare. 'Well?' he said.

'I fear your friend will not waken again,' answered the Chinese. 'I made him a little more comfortable.'

*But lying strapped on an improvised litter between two ponies, unconscious. . . . Yes, concussion, when they clubbed him last night. A Patrol hospital could put him to rights soon enough. But the nearest Patrol office is in Cambaluc, and I can't see Toktai letting me go back to the scooter and use its radio. John Sandoval is going to die here, six hundred and fifty years before he was born.*

Everard looked into cool brown eyes, interested, not unsympathetic, but alien to him. It was no use, he knew; arguments which were logical in his culture were gibberish today; but one had to try. 'Can you, at least, not make Toktai understand what ruin he is to bring on himself, on his whole people, by this?'

Li stroked his fork beard. 'It is plain to see, honoured sir, your nation has arts unknown to us,' he said. 'But what of it? The barbarians —' he gave Everard's Mongol guards a quick glance, but evidently they didn't understand the Sung Chinese he used – 'took many kingdoms superior to them in every way but fighting skill. Now already we know that you, ah, amended the truth when you spoke of a hostile empire near these lands. Why should your king try to frighten us away with a falsehood, did he not have reason to fear us?'

Everard spoke with care: 'Our glorious emperor dislikes bloodshed. But if you force him to strike you down —'

'Please.' Li looked pained. He waved one slender hand, as if brushing off an insect. 'Say what you will to Toktai, and I shall not interfere. It would not sadden me to return home; I came only under Imperial orders. But let us two, speaking confidentially, not insult each other's intelligence. Do you not see, eminent lord, that there is no possible harm with which you can threaten these men? Death they despise; even the most lingering torture must kill them in time; even the most disgraceful mutilation can be made as naught by a man willing to bite through his tongue and die. Toktai sees eternal shame if he turns back at this stage of events, and a good chance of eternal glory and uncountable wealth if he continues.'

Everard sighed. His own humiliating capture had indeed been the turning point. The Mongols had been very near bolting at the thunder show. Many had grovelled and wailed (and from now on would be all the more aggressive, to erase that memory). Toktai charged the source as much in horror as defiance; a few men and horses had been able to come along. Li himself was partly responsible; scholar, sceptic, familiar with sleight-of-hand and pyrotechnic displays, the Chinese had helped hearten Toktai to attack before one of those thunderbolts did strike home.

*The truth of the matter is, son, we misjudged these people. We should have taken along a Specialist, who'd have an intuitive feeling for the nuances of this culture. But no, we assumed a brainful of facts would be enough. Now what? A Patrol relief expedition may show up eventually, but Jack will be dead in another day or two. . . .* Everard looked at the stony warrior face on his left. *Quite probably I'll be dead also. They're still on edge. They'd sooner scrag me than not.*

And even if he should (unlikely chance!) survive to be hauled out of this mess by another Patrol band – it would be tough to face his comrades. An Unattached agent, with all the special privileges of his rank, was expected to handle situations without extra help. Without leading valuable men to their deaths.

'So I advise you most sincerely not to attempt any more deceptions.'

'What?' Everard turned back to Li.

'You do understand, do you not,' said the Chinese, 'that our native guides did flee? That you are now taking their place? But we expect to meet other tribes before long, establish communication . . .'

Everard nodded a throbbing head. The sunlight pierced his eyes. He was not astonished at the ready Mongol progress through scores of separate language areas. If you aren't fussy about grammar, a few hours suffice to pick up the small number of basic words and gestures; thereafter you can take days or weeks actually learning to speak with your hired escort.

'. . . and obtain guides from stage to stage, as we did before,' continued Li. 'Any misdirection you may have given will soon be apparent. Toktai will punish it in most uncivilized ways. On the other hand, faithful service will be rewarded. You may hope in time to rise high in the provincial court, after the conquest.'

Everard sat unmoving. The casual boast was like an explosion in his mind.

He had been assuming the Patrol would send another force. Obviously *something* was going to prevent Toktai's return. But was it so obvious? Why had this interference been ordered at all, if there were not – in some paradoxical way his twentieth-century logic couldn't grasp – an uncertainty, a shakiness in the continuum right at this point?

Judas in hell! Perhaps the Mongol expedition was going to succeed! Perhaps all the future of an American Khanate which Sandoval had not quite dared dream of ... was the real future.

There are quirks and discontinuities in space-time. The world lines can double back and bite themselves off, so that things and events appear causelessly, meaningless flutters soon lost and forgotten. Such as Manse Everard, marooned in the past with a dead John Sandoval, after coming from a future that never existed as the agent of a Time Patrol which never was.


7


At sundown their unmerciful pace had brought the expedition into sagebrush and greasewood country. The hills were steep and brown; dust smoked under hoofs; silvery-green bushes grew sparse, sweetening the air when bruised but offering little else.

Everard helped lay Sandoval on the ground. The Navajo's eyes were closed, his face sunken and hot. Sometimes he tossed and muttered a bit. Everard squeezed water from a wetted cloth past the cracked lips, but could do nothing more.

The Mongols established themselves more gaily than of late. They had overcome two great sorcerers and suffered no further attack, and the implications were growing upon them. They went about their chores chattering to each other, and after a frugal meal they broke out the leather bags of *kumiss.*

Everard remained with Sandoval, near the middle of camp. Two guards had been posted on him, who sat with strung bows a few yards away but didn't talk. Now and then one of them would get up to tend the small fire. Presently silence fell on their comrades too. Even this leathery host was tired; men rolled up and went to sleep, the outposts rode their rounds drowsy-eyed, other watch-fires burned to embers while stars kindled overhead, a coyote yelped across miles. Everard covered Sandoval against the gathering cold; his own low flames showed rime frost on sage leaves. He huddled into a cloak and wished his captors would at least give him back his pipe.

A footfall crunched dry soil. Everard's guards snatched arrows for their bows. Toktai moved into the light, his head bare above a mantle. The guards bent low and moved back into shadow.

Toktai halted. Everard looked up and then down again. The Noyon stared a while at Sandoval. Finally, most gently, he said: 'I do not think your friend will live to next sunset.'

Everard grunted.

'Have you any medicines which might help?' asked Toktai. 'There are some queer things in your saddlebags.'

'I have a remedy against infection, and another against pain,' said Everard mechanically. 'But for a cracked skull, he must be taken to skilful physicians.'

Toktai sat down and held his hands to the fire. 'I'm sorry we have no surgeons along.'

'You could let us go,' said Everard without hope. 'My chariot, back at the last camp, could get him to help in time.'

'Now you know I can't do that!' Toktai chuckled. His pity for the dying man flickered out. 'After all, Eburar, you started the trouble.'

Since it was true, the Patrolman made no retort.

'I don't hold it against you,' went on Toktai. 'In fact, I'm still anxious to be friends. If I weren't, I'd stop for a few days and wring all you know out of you.'

Everard flared up. 'You could try!'

'And succeed, I think, with a man who has to carry medicine against pain.' Toktai's grin was wolfish. 'However, you may be useful as a hostage or something. And I do like your nerve. I'll even tell you an idea I have. I think maybe you don't belong to this rich southland at all. I think you're an adventurer, one of a little band of shamans. You have the southern king in your power, or hope to, and don't want strangers interfering.' Toktai spat into the fire. 'There are old stories about that sort of thing, and finally a hero overthrew the wizard. Why not me?'

Everard sighed. 'You will learn why not, Noyon.' He wondered how correct that was.

'Oh, now.' Toktai clapped him on the back. 'Can't you tell me even a little? There's no blood feud between us. Let's be friends.'

Everard jerked a thumb at Sandoval.

'It's a shame, that,' said Toktai, 'but he would keep on resisting an officer of the Kha Khan. Come, let's have a drink together, Eburar. I'll send a man for a bag.'

The Patrolman made a face. 'That's no way to pacify me!'

'Oh, your people don't like *kumiss*? I'm afraid it's all we have. We drank up our wine long ago.'

'You could let me have my whisky.' Everard looked at Sandoval again, and out into night, and felt the cold creep inward. 'God, but I could use that!'

'Eh?'

'A drink of our own. We had some in our saddlebags.'

'Well . . .' Toktai hesitated. 'Very well. Come along and we'll fetch it.'

The guards followed their chief and their prisoner, through the brush and the sleeping warriors, up to a pile of assorted gear also under guard. One of the latter sentries ignited a stick in his fire to give Everard some light. The Patrolman's back muscles tensed – arrows were aimed at him now, drawn to the barb – but he squatted and went through his own stuff, careful not to move fast. When he had both canteens of Scotch, he returned to his own place.

Toktai sat down across the fire. He watched Everard pour a shot into the canteen cap and toss it off. 'Smells odd,' he said.

'Try.' The Patrolman handed over the canteen.

It was an impulse of sheer loneliness. Toktai wasn't such a bad sort. Not in his own terms. And when you sit by your dying partner, you'd booze with the devil himself, just to keep from thinking. The Mongol sniffed dubiously, looked back at Everard, paused, and then raised the bottle to his lips with a bravura gesture.

'*Whoo-oo-oo!*'

Everard scrambled to catch the flask before too much was spilled. Toktai gasped and spat. One guardsman nocked an arrow, the other sprang to lay a hard hand on Everard's shoulder. A sword gleamed high. 'It's not poison!' the Patrolman exclaimed. 'It's only too strong for him. See, I'll drink some more myself.'

Toktai waved the guards back and glared from watery eyes. 'What do you make that of?' he choked. 'Dragon's blood?'

'Barley.' Everard didn't feel like explaining distillation. He poured himself another slug. 'Go ahead, drink your mare's milk.'

Toktai smacked his lips. 'It does warm you up, doesn't it? Like pepper.' He reached out a grimy hand. 'Give me some more.'

Everard sat still for a few seconds. 'Well?' growled Toktai.

The Patrolman shook his head. 'I told you, it's too strong for Mongols.'

'What? See here, you whey-faced son of a Turk —'

'On your head be it, then. I warn you fairly, with your men here as witnesses, you will be sick tomorrow.'

Toktai guzzled heartily, belched, and passed the canteen back. 'Nonsense. I simply wasn't prepared for it, the first time. Drink up!'

Everard took his time. Toktai grew impatient. 'Hurry along there. No, give me the other flask.'

'Very well. You are the chief. But I beg you, don't try to match me draught for draught. You can't do it.'

'What do you mean, I can't do it? Why, I've drunk twenty men senseless in Karakorum. None of your gutless Chinks, either: they were all Mongols.' Toktai poured down a couple of ounces more.

Everard sipped with care. But he hardly felt the effect anyway, save as a burning along his gullet. He was too tightly strung. Suddenly he was glimpsing what might be a way out.

'Here, it's a cold night,' he said, and offered his canteen to the nearest guardsman. 'You lads have one to keep you warm.'

Toktai looked up, a trifle muzzily. 'Good stuff, this,' he objected. 'Too good for . . .' He remembered himself and snapped his words off short. Cruel and absolute the Mongol Empire might be, but officers shared equally with the humblest of their men.

The warrior grabbed the jug, giving his chief a resentful look, and slanted it to his mouth. 'Easy, there,' said Everard. 'It's heady.'

'Nothin's heady to me.' Toktai poured a further dose into himself. 'Sober as a bonze.' He wagged his finger. 'That's the trouble bein' a Mongol. You're so hardy you can't get drunk.'

'Are you bragging or complaining?' said Everard. The first warrior fanned his tongue, resumed a stance of alertness, and passed the bottle to his companion. Toktai hoisted the other canteen again.

'Ahhh!' He stared, owlish. 'That was fine. Well, better get to sleep now. Give him back his liquor, men.'

Everard's throat tightened. But he managed to leer. 'Yes, thanks, I'll want some more,' he said. 'I'm glad you realize you can't take it.'

'Wha'd'you mean?' Toktai glared at him. 'No such thing as too much. Not for a Mongol!' He glugged afresh. The first guardsman received the other flask and took a hasty snort before it should be too late.

Everard sucked in a shaken breath. It might work out after all. It might.

Toktai was used to carousing. There was no doubt that he or his men could handle *kumiss*, wine, ale, mead, *kvass*, that thin beer miscalled rice wine – any beverage of this era. They'd know when they'd had enough, say goodnight, and walk a straight line to their bedrolls. The trouble was, no substance merely fermented can get over about 24 proof – the process is stopped by its waste product – and most of what they brewed in the thirteenth century ran well under 5 per cent alcohol, with a high foodstuff content to boot.

Scotch whisky is in quite a different class. If you try to drink that like beer, or even like wine, you are in trouble.

Your judgment will be gone before you've noticed its absence, and consciousness follows soon after.

Everard reached for the canteen held by one of the guards. 'Give me that!' he said. 'You'll drink it all up!'

The warrior grinned and took another long gulp, before passing it on to his fellow. Everard stood up and made an undignified scrabble for it. A guard poked him in the stomach. He went over on his backside. The Mongols bawled laughter, leaning on each other. So good a joke called for another drink.

When Toktai folded, Everard alone noticed. The Noyon slid from a cross-legged to a recumbent position. The fire sputtered up long enough to show a silly smile on his face. Everard squatted wire-tense.

The end of one sentry came a few minutes later. He reeled, went on all fours, and began to jettison his dinner. The other turned, blinking, fumbling after a sword. 'Wha's mattuh?' he groaned. 'Wha' yuh done? Poison?'

Everard moved.

He had hopped over the fire and fallen on Toktai before the last guard realized it. The Mongol stumbled forward, crying out. Everard found Toktai's sword. It flashed from the scabbard as he bounced up. The warrior got his own blade aloft. Everard didn't like to kill a nearly helpless man. He stepped close, knocked the other weapon aside, and his fist clopped. The Mongol sank to his knees, retched, and slept.

Everard bounded away. Men stirred in the dark, calling. He heard hoofs drum, one of the mounted sentries racing to investigate. Somebody took a brand from an almost extinct fire and whirled it till it flared. Everard went flat on his belly.

A warrior pelted by, not seeing him in the brush. He glided towards deeper darkness. A yell behind him, a machine-gun volley of curses, told that someone had found the Noyon.

Everard stood up and began to run.

The horses had been hobbled and turned out under guard as usual. They were a dark mass on the plain, which lay grey-white beneath a sky crowded with sharp stars. Everard saw one of the Mongol watchers gallop to meet him. A voice barked: 'What's happening?'

He pitched his answer high. 'Attack on camp!' It was only to gain time, lest the horseman recognize him and fire an arrow. He crouched, visible as a hunched and cloaked shape. The Mongol reined in with a spurt of dust. Everard sprang.

He got hold of the pony's bridle before he was recognized. Then the sentry yelled and drew sword. He hewed downward. But Everard was on the left side. The blow from above came awkwardly, easily parried. Everard chopped in return and felt his edge go into meat. The horse reared in alarm. Its rider fell from the saddle. He rolled over and staggered up again, bellowing. Everard already had one foot in a panshaped stirrup. The Mongol limped towards him, blood running black in that light from a wounded leg. Everard mounted and laid the flat of his own blade on the horse's crupper.

He got going towards the herd. Another rider pounded to intercept him. Everard ducked. An arrow buzzed where he had been. The stolen pony plunged, fighting its unfamiliar burden. Everard needed a minute to get it under control again. The archer might have taken him then, by coming up and going at it hand to hand. But habit sent the man past at a gallop, shooting. He missed in the dimness. Before he could turn, Everard was out of night view.

The Patrolman uncoiled a lariat at the saddlebow and broke into the skittish herd. He roped the nearest animal, which accepted it with blessed meakness. Leaning over, he slashed the hobbles with his sword and rode off, leading the remount. They came out the other side of the herd and started north.

*A stern chase is a long chase,* Everard told himself inappropriately. *But they're bound to overhaul me if I don't lose 'em. Let's see, if I remember my geography, the lava beds lie north-west of here.*

He cast a glance behind. No one pursued yet. They'd need a while to organize themselves. However . . .

Thin lightnings winked from above. The cloven air boomed behind them. He felt a chill, deeper than the night cold. But he eased his pace. There was no more reason for hurry. That must be Manse Everard —

— who had returned to the Patrol vehicle and ridden it south in space and backward in time to this same instant.

That was cutting it fine, he thought. Patrol doctrine

frowned on helping oneself thus. Too much danger of a closed causal loop, or of tangling past and future.

*But in this case, I'll get away with it. No reprimands, even. Because it's to rescue Jack Sandoval, not myself. I've already got free. I could shake pursuit in the mountains, which I know and the Mongols don't. The time-hopping is only to save my friend's life.*

*Besides* (an upsurging bitterness) *what's this whole mission been, except the future doubling back to create its own past? Without us, the Mongols might well have taken over America, and then there'd never have been any us.*

The sky was enormous, crystalline black; you rarely saw that many stars. The Great Bear flashed above hoar earth; hoofbeats rang through silence. Everard had not felt so alone before now.

'And what am I doing back there?' he asked aloud.

The answer came to him, and he eased a little, fell into the rhythm of his horses and started eating miles. He wanted to get this over with. But what he must do turned out to be less bad than he had feared.

Toktai and Li Tai-Tsung never came home. But that was not because they perished at sea or in the forests. It was because a sorcerer rode down from heaven and killed all their horses with thunderbolts, and smashed and burned their ships in the river mouth. No Chinese sailor would venture on to those tricky seas in whatever clumsy vessel could be built here; no Mongol would think it possible to go home on foot. Indeed, it probably wasn't. The expedition would stay, marry into the Indians, live out their days. Chinook, Tlingit, Nootka, all the potlatch tribes, with their big seagoing canoes, lodges and copperworking, furs and cloths and haughtiness ... well, a Mongol Noyon, even a Confucian scholar might live less happily and usefully than in creating such a life for such a race.

Everard nodded to himself. So much for that. What was harder to take than the thwarting of Toktai's bloodthirsty ambitions was the truth about his own corps; which was his own family and nation and reason for living. The distant supermen turned out to be not quite such idealists after all. They weren't merely safeguarding a perhaps divinely ordained history which led to them. Here and there they, too, meddled, to create their own past. . . . Don't ask if there ever was any 'original' scheme of things. Keep your mind shut. Regard the rutted road mankind had to travel, and tell yourself that if it could be better in places, in other places it could be worse.

'It may be a crooked game,' said Everard, 'but it's the only one in town.'

His voice came so loud, in that huge rime-white land, that he didn't speak any more. He clucked at his horse and rode a little faster northward.

# DELENDA EST

## I

THE HUNTING is good in Europe twenty thousand years ago, and the winter sports are unexcelled anywhen. So the Time Patrol, always solicitous for its highly trained personnel, maintains a lodge in the Pleistocene Pyrenees.

Manse Everard stood on a glassed-in verandah and looked across ice-blue distances towards the northern slopes where the mountains fell off into woodland, marsh, and tundra. His big body was clad in loose green trousers and tunic of twenty-third-century insulsynth, boots hand-made by a nineteenth-century French-Canadian; he smoked a foul old briar of indeterminate origin. There was a vague restlessness about him, and he ignored the noise from within, where half a dozen agents were drinking and talking and playing the piano.

A Cro-Magnon guide went by across the snow-covered yard, a tall handsome fellow dressed rather like an Eskimo (why had romance never credited paleolithic man with enough sense to wear jacket, pants, and footgear in a glacial period?), his face painted, one of the steel knives which had hired him at his belt. The Patrol could act quite freely, this far back in time; there was no danger of upsetting the past, for the metal would rust away and the strangers be forgotten in a few centuries. The main nuisance was that female agents from the more libertine periods upstairs were always having affairs with the native hunters.

Piet van Sarawak (Dutch-Indonesian-Venusian, early twenty-fourth AD), a slim, dark young man whose looks and technique gave the guides some stiff competition, joined Everard. They stood for a moment in companionable silence. He was also Unattached, on call to help out in any milieu, and had worked with the American before. They had taken their vacation together.

He spoke first, in Temporal. 'I hear they've spotted a few

mammoths near Toulouse.' The city would not be built for a long while yet, but habit was powerful.

'I've bagged one,' said Everard impatiently. 'I've also been skiing and mountain-climbing and watched the native dances.'

Van Sarawak nodded, took out a cigarette, and puffed it into lighting. The bones stood out in his lean brown face as he sucked the smoke inward. 'A pleasant loafing spell, this,' he agreed, 'but after a bit the outdoor life begins to pall.'

There were still two weeks of their furlough. In theory, since he could return almost to the moment of departure, an agent could take indefinite vacations; but actually he was supposed to devote a certain percentage of his probable lifetime to the job (They never told you when you were scheduled to die, and you had better sense than to try finding out for yourself. It wouldn't have been certain anyhow, time being mutable. One perquisite of an agent's office was the Danellian longevity treatment.)

'What I would enjoy,' continued Van Sarawak, 'is some bright lights, music, girls who've never heard of time travel —'

'Done!' said Everard.

'Augustan Rome?' asked the other eagerly. 'I've never been there. I could get a hypno on language and customs here.'

Everard shook his head. 'It's overrated. Unless we want to go 'way upstairs, the most glorious decadence available is right in my own milieu. New York, say. . . . If you know the right phone numbers, and I do.'

Van Sarawak chuckled. 'I know a few places in my own sector,' he replied, 'but by and large, a pioneer society has little use for the finer arts of amusement. Very good, let's be off to New York, in – when?'

'Make it 1960. That was the last time I was there, in my public *persona*, before coming here-now.'

They grinned at each other and went off to pack. Everard had foresightedly brought along some mid-twentieth garments in his friend's size.

Throwing clothes and razor into a small suitcase, the American wondered if he could keep up with Van Sarawak. He had never been a high-powered roisterer, and wouldn't have known how to buckle a swash anywhere in spacetime. A good book, a bull session, a case of beer – that was about his speed. But even the soberest men must kick over the traces occasionally.

Or a little more than that, if he was an Unattached agent of the Time Patrol; if his job with the Engineering Studies Company was only a blind for his wanderings and warrings through all history; if he had seen that history rewritten in minor things – not by God, which would have been endurable, but by mortal and fallible men – for even the Danellians were somewhat less than God; if he was for ever haunted by the possibility of a major change, such that he and his entire world would never have existed at all. . . . Everard's battered, homely face screwed into a grimace. He ran a hand through his stiff brown hair, as if to brush the idea away. Useless to think about. Language and logic broke down in the face of the paradox. Better to relax at such moments as he could.

He picked up the suitcase and went to join Piet van Sarawak.

Their little two-piece antigravity scooter waited on its skids in the garage. You wouldn't believe, to look at it, that the controls could be set for any place on Earth and any moment of time. But an aeroplane is wonderful too, or a ship, or a fire.

> *Auprès de ma blonde*
> *Qu'il fait bon, fait bon, fait bon,*
> *Auprès de ma blonde*
> *Qu'il fait bon dormir!*

Van Sarawak sang it aloud, his breath steaming from him in the frosty air as he hopped on to the rear saddle. He'd picked up the song once when accompanying the army of Louis XIV. Everard laughed. 'Down, boy!'

'Oh, come, now,' warbled the younger man. 'It is a beautiful continuum, a gay and gorgeous cosmos. Hurry up this machine.'

Everard was not so sure; he had seen enough human misery in all the ages. You got case-hardened after a while, but down underneath, when a peasant stared at you with sick brutalized eyes, or a soldier screamed with a pike through him, or a city went up in radioactive flame, something wept. He could understand the fanatics who had tried to change events. It was only that their work was so unlikely to make anything better. . . .

He set the controls for the Engineering Studies warehouse, a good confidential place to emerge. Thereafter they'd go to his apartment, and then the fun could start.

'I trust you've said goodbye to all your lady friends here,' Everard remarked.

'Oh, most gallantly, I assure you. Come along there. You're as slow as molasses on Pluto. For your information, this vehicle does not have to be rowed home.'

Everard shrugged and threw the main switch. The garage blinked out of sight.

2

For a moment, shock held them unstirring.

The scene registered in bits and pieces. They had materialized a few inches above ground level – the scooter was designed never to come out inside a solid object – and since that was unexpected, they hit the pavement with a teeth-rattling bump. They were in some kind of square. Nearby a fountain jetted, its stone basin carved with intertwining vines. Around the plaza, streets led off between squarish buildings six to ten stories high, of brick or concrete, wildly painted and ornamented. There were automobiles, big clumsy-looking things of no recognizable type, and a crowd of people.

'Jumping gods!' Everard glared at the meters. The scooter had landed them in lower Manhattan, 23 October, 1960, at 11.30 am and the spatial coordinates of the warehouse. But there was a blustery wind throwing dust and soot in his face, the smell of chimneys, and . . .

Van Sarawak's sonic stunner jumped into his fist. The crowd was milling away from them, shouting in some babble they couldn't understand. It was a mixed lot: tall, fair round-heads, with a great deal of red hair; a number of Amerinds; half-breeds in all combinations. The men wore loose colourful blouses, tartan kilts, a sort of Scotch bonnet, shoes and knee-length stockings. Their hair was long and many favoured drooping moustaches. The women had full skirts reaching to the ankles and tresses coiled under hooded cloaks. Both sexes went in for massive bracelets and necklaces.

'What happened?' whispered the Venusian. 'Where are we?'

Everard sat rigid. His mind clicked over, whirling through all the eras he had known or read about. Industrial culture – those looked like steam cars, but why the sharp prows and figureheads? – coal-burning – postnuclear Reconstruction? No, they hadn't worn kilts then, and they had spoken English. . . .

It didn't fit. There was no such milieu recorded.

'We're getting out of here!'

His hands were on the controls when the large man jumped him. They went over on the pavement in a rage of fists and feet. Van Sarawak fired and sent someone else down unconscious; then he was seized from behind. The mob piled on top of them both, and things became hazy.

Everard had a confused impression of men in shining coppery breastplates and helmets, who shoved a billy-swinging way through the riot. He was fished out and supported in his grogginess while handcuffs were snapped on his wrists. Then he and Van Sarawak were searched and hustled off to a big enclosed vehicle. The Black Maria is much the same in all times.

He didn't come back to full consciousness until they were in a damp and chilly cell with an iron-barred door.

'Name of a flame!' The Venusian slumped on a wooden cot and put his face in his hands.

Everard stood at the door, looking out. All he could see was a narrow concrete hall and the cell across it. The map of Ireland stared cheerfully through those bars and called something unintelligible.

'What's going on?' Van Sarawak's slim body shuddered.

'I don't know,' said Everard very slowly. 'I just don't know. That machine was supposed to be foolproof, but maybe we're bigger fools than they allowed for.'

'There's no such place as this,' said Van Sarawak desperately. 'A dream?' He pinched himself and managed a rueful smile. His lip was cut and swelling, and he had the start of a gorgeous shiner. 'Logically, my friend, a pinch is no test of reality, but it has a certain reassuring effect.'

'I wish it didn't,' said Everard.

He grabbed the bars so hard they rattled. 'Could the controls have been askew, in spite of everything? Is there any city, anywhere on Earth – because I'm damned sure this is Earth, at least – any city, however obscure, which was ever like this?'

'Not to my knowledge.'

Everard hung on to his sanity and rallied all the mental training the Patrol had ever given him. That included total recall; and he had studied history, even the history of ages he had never seen, with a thoroughness that should have earned him several PhDs.

'No,' he said at last. 'Kilted brachycephalic whites, mixed up with Indians and using steam-drive automobiles, haven't happened.'

'Coordinator Stantel V,' said Van Sarawak faintly. 'In the thirty-eighth century. The Great Experimenter – colonies reproducing past societies —'

'Not any like this,' said Everard.

The truth was growing in him, and he would have traded his soul for things to be otherwise. It took all the strength he had to keep from screaming and bashing his brains out against the wall.

'We'll have to see,' he said in a flat tone.

A policeman (Everard assumed they were in the hands of the law) brought them a meal and tried to talk to them. Van Sarawak said the language sounded Celtic, but he couldn't make out more than few words. The meal wasn't bad.

Towards evening, they were led off to a washroom and got cleaned up under official guns. Everard studied the weapons; eight-shot revolvers and long-barrelled rifles. There were gas lights, whose brackets repeated the motif of wreathing vines and snakes. The facilities and firearms, as well as the smell, suggested a technology roughly equivalent to the earlier nineteenth century.

On the way back he spied a couple of signs on the walls. The script was obviously Semitic, but though Van Sarawak had some knowledge of Hebrew through dealing with the Israeli colonies on Venus, he couldn't read it.

Locked in again, they saw the other prisoners led off to do their own washing: a surprisingly merry crowd of bums, toughs, and drunks. 'Seems we get special treatment,' remarked Van Sarawak.

'Hardly astonishing,' said Everard. 'What would you do with total strangers who appeared out of nowhere and used unheard-of weapons?'

Van Sarawak's face turned to him with an unwonted grimness. 'Are you thinking what I'm thinking?' he asked.

'Probably.'

The Venusian's mouth twisted, and horror rode his voice: 'Another time line. Somebody *has* managed to change history.'

Everard nodded.

They spent an unhappy night. It would have been a boon to sleep, but the other cells were too noisy. Discipline seemed to be lax here. Also, there were bedbugs.

After a bleary breakfast, Everard and Van Sarawak were allowed to wash again and shave with safety razors not unlike the familiar type. Then a ten-man guard marched them into an office and planted itself around the walls.

They sat down before a desk and waited. The furniture was as disquietingly half-homelike, half-alien, as everything else. It was some time before the big wheels showed up. There were two: a white-haired, ruddy-cheeked man in cuirass and green tunic, presumably the chief of police, and a lean, hard-faced half-breed, grey-haired but black-moustached, wearing a blue tunic, a tam o'shanter, and on his left breast a golden bull's head which seemed an insigne of rank. He would have had a certain aquiline dignity had it not been for the thin hairy legs beneath his kilt. He was followed by two younger men, armed and uniformed much like himself, who took up their places behind him as he sat down.

Everard leaned over and whispered: 'The military, I'll bet. We seem to be of interest.'

Van Sarawak nodded sickly.

The police chief cleared his throat with conscious importance and said something to the – general? The latter answered impatiently, and addressed himself to the prisoners.

126

He barked his words out with a clarity that helped Everard get the phonemes, but with a manner that was not exactly reassuring.

Somewhere along the line, communication would have to be established. Everard pointed to himself. 'Manse Everard,' he said. Van Sarawak followed the lead and introduced himself similarly.

The general started and went into a huddle with the chief. Turning back, he snapped, '*Yrn Cimberland?*'

'No spikka da Inglees,' said Everard.

'*Gothland? Svea? Nairoin Teutonach?*'

'Those names – if they are names – they sound Germanic, don't they?' muttered Van Sarawak.

'So do our names, come to think of it,' answered Everard tautly. 'Maybe they think we're Germans.' To the general: '*Sprechen sie Deutsch?*' Blankness rewarded him. '*Taler ni svensk? Niederlands? Dönsk tunga? Parlez-vous français?* Goddamit, *habla usted español?*'

The police chief cleared his throat again and pointed to himself. 'Cadwallader Mac Barça,' he said. 'The general hight Cynyth ap Ceorn.' Or so, at least, Everard's Anglo-Saxon mind interpreted the noises picked up by his ears.

'Celtic, all right,' he said. Sweat prickled under his arms. 'But just to make sure. . . .' He pointed inquiringly at a few other men, being rewarded with monickers like Hamilcar ap Angus, Asshur yr Cathlann, and Finn O'Carthia. 'No . . . there's a distinct Semitic element here too. That fits in with their alphabet.'

Van Sarawak wet his lips. 'Try classical languages,' he urged harshly. 'Maybe we can find out where this history went insane.'

'*Loquerisne latine?*' That drew a blank. 'Ελλευιζεις?'

General ap Ceorn jerked, blew out his moustache, and narrowed his eyes. '*Hellenach?*' he demanded. '*Yrn Parthia?*'

Everard shook his head. 'They've at least heard of Greek,' he said slowly. He tried a few more words, but no one knew the tongue.

Ap Ceorn growled something to one of his men, who bowed and went out. There was a long silence.

Everard found himself losing personal fear. He was in a bad spot, yes, and might not live very long; but whatever

127

happened to him was ludicrously unimportant compared to what had been done to the entire world.

God in Heaven! To the universe!

He couldn't grasp it. Sharp in his mind rose the land he knew, broad plains and tall mountains and prideful cities. There was the grave image of his father, and yet he remembered being a small child and lifted up skyward while his father laughed beneath him. And his mother ... they had a good life together, those two.

There had been a girl he knew in college, the sweetest little wench a man could ever have been privileged to walk in the rain with; and Bernie Aaronson, the nights of beer and smoke and talk; Phil Brackney, who had picked him out of the mud in France when machine guns were raking a ruined field; Charlie and Mary Whitcomb, high tea and a low cannel fire in Victoria's London; Keith and Cynthia Denison in their chrome-plated eyrie above New York; Jack Sandoval among tawny Arizona crags; a dog he had once had; the austere cantos of Dante and the ringing thunder of Shakespeare; the glory which was York Minster and the Golden Gate Bridge – Christ, a man's life, and the lives of who knew how many billions of human creatures, toiling and enduring and laughing and going down into dust to make room for their sons. ... It had never been.

He shook his head, dazed with grief, and sat devoid of real understanding.

The soldiers came back with a map and spread it out on the desk. Ap Ceorn gestured curtly, and Everard and Van Sarawak bent over it.

Yes, Earth, a Mercator projection, though eidetic memory showed that the mapping was rather crude. The continents and islands were there in bright colours, but the nations were something else.

'Can you read those names, Van?'

'I can make a guess, on the basis of the Hebraic alphabet,' said the Venusian. He began to read out the words. Ap Ceorn grunted and corrected him.

North America down to about Colombia was Ynys yr Afallon, seemingly one country divided into states. South America was a big realm, Huy Braseal, and some smaller countries whose names looked Indian. Australasia, Indone-

sia, Borneo, Burma, eastern India, and a good deal of the
Pacific belonged to Hinduraj. Afghanistan and the rest of
India were Punjab. Han included China, Korea, Japan, and
eastern Siberia. Littorn owned the rest of Russia and reached
well into Europe. The British Isles were Brittys; France and
the Low Countries were Gallis; the Iberian peninsula was
Celtan. Central Europe and the Balkans were divided into
many small nations, some of which had Hunnish-looking
names. Switzerland and Austria made up Helveti; Italy was
Cimberland; the Scandinavian peninsula was split down the
middle, Svea in the north and Gothland in the south. North
Africa looked like a confederacy, reaching from Senegal to
Suez and nearly to the equator, under the name of Carthagalann; the southern part of the continent was partitioned
among minor sovereignties, many of which had purely
African titles. The Near East held Parthia and Arabia.

Van Sarawak looked up. He had tears in his eyes.

Ap Ceorn snarled a question and waved his finger about.
He wanted to know where they were from.

Everard shrugged and pointed skyward. The one thing he
could not admit was the truth. He and Van Sarawak had
agreed to claim they were from another planet, since this
world hardly had space travel.

Ap Ceorn spoke to the chief, who nodded and replied. The
prisoners were returned to their cell.

### 3

'And now what?' Van Sarawak slumped on his cot and
stared at the floor.

'We play along,' said Everard greyly. 'We do anything to
get at our scooter and escape. Once we're free, we can take
stock.'

'But what happened?'

'I don't know, I tell you! Offhand, it looks as if something
upset the Graeco-Romans and the Celts took over, but I
couldn't say what it was.' Everard prowled the room. A
bitter determination was growing in him.

'Remember your basic theory,' he said. 'Events are the
result of a complex. There are no single causes. That's why

it's so hard to change history. If I went back to, say, the Middle Ages, and shot one of FDR's Dutch forebears, he'd still be born in the late nineteenth century – because he and his genes resulted from the entire world of his ancestors, and there'd have been compensation. But every so often, a really key event does occur. Some one happening is a nexus of so many world lines that its outcome is decisive for the whole future.

'Somehow, for some reason, somebody has ripped up one of those events, back in the past.'

'No more Hesperus City,' mumbled Van Sarawak. 'No more sitting by the canals in the blue twilight, no more Aphrodite vintages, no more – did you know I had a sister on Venus?'

'Shut up!' Everard almost shouted it. 'I know. To hell with that. What counts is what we can do.

'Look,' he went on after a moment, 'the Patrol and the Danellians are wiped out. (Don't ask me why they weren't "always" wiped out; why this is the first time we came back from the far past to find a changed future. I don't understand the mutable-time paradoxes. We just did, that's all.) But anyhow, such of the Patrol offices and resorts as antedate the switchpoint won't have been affected. There must be a few hundred agents we can rally.'

'If we can get back to them.'

'We can then find the key event and stop whatever interference there was with it. We've got to!'

'A pleasant thought. But . . .'

Feet tramped outside. A key clicked in the lock. The prisoners backed away. Then, all at once, Van Sarawak was bowing and beaming and spilling gallantries. Even Everard had to gape.

The girl who entered in front of three soldiers was a knockout. She was tall, with a sweep of rusty-red hair past her shoulders to the slim waist; her eyes were green and alight, her face came from all the Irish colleens who had ever lived; the long white dress was snug around a figure meant to stand on the walls of Troy. Everard noticed vaguely that this timeline used cosmetics, but she had small need of them. He paid no attention to the gold and amber of her jewellery, or to the guns behind her.

She smiled, a little timidly, and spoke: 'Can you understand me? It was thought you might know Greek.'

Her language was classical rather than modern. Everard, who had once had a job in Alexandrine times, could follow it through her accent if he paid close heed – which was inevitable anyway.

'Indeed I do,' he replied, his words stumbling over each other in their haste to get out.

'What are you snakkering?' demanded Van Sarawak.

'Ancient Greek,' said Everard.

'It would be,' mourned the Venusian. His despair seemed to have vanished, and his eyes bugged.

Everard introduced himself and his companion. The girl said her name was Deirdre Mac Morn. 'Oh, no,' groaned Van Sarawak. 'This is too much. Manse, teach me Greek. Fast.'

'Shut up,' said Everard. 'This is serious business.'

'Well, but can't I have some of the business?'

Everard ignored him and invited the girl to sit down. He joined her on a cot, while the other Patrolman hovered unhappily by. The guards kept their weapons ready.

'Is Greek still a living language?' asked Everard.

'Only in Parthia, and there it is most corrupt,' said Deirdre. 'I am a classical scholar, among other things. *Saorann* ap Ceorn is my uncle, so he asked me to see if I could talk with you. Not many in Afallon know the Attic tongue.'

'Well —' Everard suppressed a silly grin – 'I am most grateful to your uncle.'

Her eyes rested gravely on him. 'Where are you from? And how does it happen that you speak only Greek, of all known languages?'

'I speak Latin too.'

'Latin?' She frowned in thought. 'Oh, the Roman speech, was it not? I am afraid you will find no one who knows much about it.'

'Greek will do,' said Everard firmly.

'But you have not told me whence you came,' she insisted.

Everard shrugged. 'We've not been treated very politely,' he hinted.

'I'm sorry.' It seemed genuine. 'But our people are so excitable. Especially now, with the international situation what it is. And when you two appeared out of thin air. . . .'

Everard nodded. The international situation? That had an unpleasantly familiar ring. 'What do you mean?' he inquired.

'Surely you know. With Huy Braseal and Hinduraj about to go to war, and all of us wondering what will happen. . . . It is not easy to be a small power.'

'A small power? But I saw a map. Afallon looked big enough to me.'

'We wore ourselves out two hundred years ago, in the great war with Littorn. Now none of our confederated states can agree on a single policy.' Deirdre looked directly into his eyes. 'What is this ignorance of yours?'

Everard swallowed and said, 'We're from another world.'

'What?'

'Yes. A planet (no, that means "wanderer") . . . an orb encircling Sirius. That's our name for a certain star.'

'But – what do you mean? A world attendant on a star? I cannot understand you.'

'Don't you know? A star is a sun like . . .'

Deirdre shrank back and made a sign with her finger. 'The Great Baal aid us,' she whispered. 'Either you are mad or . . . The stars are mounted in a crystal sphere.'

*Oh, no!*

'What of the wandering stars you can see?' asked Everard slowly. 'Mars and Venus and —'

'I know not those names. If you mean Moloch, Ashtoreth, and the rest, of course they are worlds like ours, attendant on the sun like our own. One holds the spirits of the dead, one is the home of witches, one . . .'

*All this and steam cars too.* Everard smiled shakily. 'If you'll not believe me, then what do you think I am?'

Deirdre regarded him with large eyes. 'I think you must be sorcerers,' she said.

There was no answer to that. Everard asked a few weak questions, but learned little more than that this city was Catuvellaunan, a trading and manufacturing centre. Deirdre estimated its population at two million, and that of all Afallon at fifty million, but wasn't sure. They didn't take censuses here.

The Patrolmen's fate was equally undetermined. Their scooter and other possessions had been sequestrated by the military, but no one dared monkey with the stuff, and treatment of the owners was being hotly debated. Everard got the impression that all government, including the leadership of the armed forces, was rather a sloppy process of individualistic wrangling. Afallon itself was the loosest of confederacies, built out of former nations – Brittic colonies and Indians who had adopted European culture – all jealous of their rights. The old Mayan Empire, destroyed in a war with Texas (Tehannach) and annexed, had not forgotten its time of glory, and sent the most rambunctious delegates of all to the Council of Suffetes.

The Mayans wanted to make an alliance with Huy Braseal, perhaps out of friendship for fellow Indians. The West Coast states, fearful of Hinduraj, were toadies of the South-east Asian empire. The Middle West (of course) was isolationist; the Eastern States were torn every which way, but inclined to follow the lead of Brittys.

When he gathered that slavery existed here, though not on racial lines, Everard wondered briefly and wildly if the time changers might not have been Dixiecrats.

Enough! He had his own neck, and Van's, to think about. 'We are from Sirius,' he declared loftily. 'Your ideas about the stars are mistaken. We came as peaceful explorers, and if we are molested, there will be others of our kind to take vengeance.'

Deirdre looked so unhappy that he felt conscience-stricken. 'Will they spare the children?' she begged. 'The children had nothing to do with it.' Everard could imagine the vision in her head, small crying captives led off to the slave markets of a world of witches.

'There need be no trouble at all if we are released and our property returned,' he said.

'I shall speak to my uncle,' she promised, 'but even if I can sway him, he is only one man on the Council. The thought of what your weapons could mean if we had them has driven men mad.'

She rose. Everard clasped both her hands – they lay warm and soft in his – and smiled crookedly at her. 'Buck up, kid,' he said in English. She shivered, pulled free of him, and made the hex sign again.

'Well,' demanded Van Sarawak when they were alone,

'what did you find out?' After being told, he stroked his chin and murmured, 'That was one glorious little collection of sinusoids. There could be worse worlds than this.'

'Or better,' said Everard roughly. 'They don't have atomic bombs, but neither do they have penicillin, I'll bet. Our job is not to play God.'

'No. No, I suppose not.' The Venusian sighed.


4


They spent a restless day. Night had fallen when lanterns glimmered in the corridor and a military guard unlocked the cell. The prisoners were led silently to a rear exit where two automobiles waited; they were put into one, and the whole troop drove off.

Catuvellaunan did not have outdoor lighting, and there wasn't much night traffic. Somehow that made the sprawling city unreal in the dark. Everard paid attention to the mechanics of his car. Steam-powered, as he had guessed, burning powdered coal; rubber-tyred wheels; a sleek body with a sharp nose and serpent figurehead; the whole simple to operate and honestly built, but not too well designed. Apparently this world had gradually developed a rule-of-thumb engineering, but no systematic science worth talking about.

They crossed a clumsy iron bridge to Long Island, here also a residential section for the well-to-do. Despite the dimness of oil-lamp headlights, their speed was high. Twice they came near having an accident: no traffic signals, and seemingly no drivers who did not hold caution in contempt.

Government and traffic ... hm. It all looked French, somehow, ignoring those rare interludes when France got a Henry of Navarre or a Charles de Gaulle. And even in Everard's own twentieth century, France was largely Celtic. He was no respecter of windy theories about inborn racial traits, but there was something to be said for traditions so ancient as to be unconscious and ineradicable. A Western world in which the Celts had become dominant, the Germanic peoples reduced to a few small outposts. ... Yes, look at the Ireland of home; or recall how tribal politics had queered Vercingetorix's revolt. . . . But what about Littorn? Wait a minute! In *his* early Middle Ages, Lithuania had been a powerful state; it had held off Germans, Poles, and Russians alike for a long time, and hadn't even taken Christianity till the fifteenth century. Without German competition, Lithuania might very well have advanced eastward. . . .

In spite of the Celtic political instability, this was a world of large states, fewer separate nations than Everard's. That argued an older society. If his own Western civilization had developed out of the decaying Roman Empire about, say, AD 600, the Celts in this world must have taken over earlier than that.

Everard was beginning to realize what had happened to Rome, but reserved his conclusions for the time being.

The cars drew up before an ornamental gate set in a long stone wall. The drivers talked with two armed guards wearing the livery of a private estate and the thin steel collars of slaves. The gate was opened and the cars went along a gravelled driveway between lawns and trees. At the far end, almost on the beach, stood a house. Everard and Van Sarawak were gestured out and led towards it.

It was a rambling wooden structure. Gas lamps on the porch showed it painted in gaudy stripes; the gables and beam-ends were carved into dragon heads. Close by he heard the sea, and there was enough light from a sinking crescent moon for Everard to make out a ship standing in close: presumably a freighter, with a tall smokestack and a figure-head.

The windows glowed yellow. A slave butler admitted the party. The interior was panelled in dark wood, also carved, the floors thickly carpeted. At the end of the hall was a living-room with overstuffed furniture, several paintings in a stiff conventionalized style, and a merry blaze in an enormous stone fireplace.

*Saorann* ap Ceorn sat in one chair, Deirdre in another. She laid aside a book as they entered and rose, smiling. The officer puffed a cigar and glowered. Some words were swapped, and the guards disappeared. The butler fetched in wine on a tray, and Deirdre invited the Patrolmen to sit down.

Everard sipped from his glass – the wine was an excellent Burgundy – and asked bluntly, 'Why are we here?'

Deirdre dazzled him with a smile. 'Surely you find it more pleasant than the jail.'

'Of course. As well as more ornamental. But I still want to know. Are we being released?'

'You are . . .' She hunted for a diplomatic answer, but there seemed to be too much frankness in her. 'You are welcome here, but may not leave the estate. We hope you can be persuaded to help us. You would be richly rewarded.'

'Help? How?'

'By showing our artisans and Druids how to make more weapons and magical carts like your own.'

Everard sighed. It was no use trying to explain. They didn't have the tools to make the tools to make what was needed, but how could he get that across to a folk who believed in witchcraft?

'Is this your uncle's home?' he asked.

'No, my own,' said Deirdre. 'I am the only child of my parents, who were wealthy nobles. They died last year.'

Ap Ceorn clipped out several words. Deirdre translated with a worried frown: 'The tale of your advent is known to all Catuvellaunan by now; and that includes the foreign spies. We hope you can remain hidden from them here.'

Everard, remembering the pranks Axis and Allies had played in little neutral nations like Portugal, shivered. Men made desperate by approaching war would not likely be as courteous as the Afallonians.

'What is this conflict going to be about?' he inquired.

'The control of the Icenian Ocean, of course. In particular, certain rich islands we call Ynys yr Lyonnach.' Deirdre got up in a single flowing movement and pointed out Hawaii on a globe. 'You see,' she went on earnestly, 'as I told you, Littorn and the western alliance – including us – wore each other out fighting. The great powers today, expanding, quarrelling, are Huy Braseal and Hinduraj. Their conflict sucks in the lesser nations, for the clash is not only between ambitions, but between systems: the monarchy of Hinduraj against the sun-worshipping theocracy of Huy Braseal.'

'What is your religion, if I may ask?'

Deirdre blinked. The question seemed almost meaningless to her. 'The more educated people think that there is a Great Baal who made all the lesser gods,' she answered at last, slowly. 'But, naturally, we maintain the ancient cults, and pay respect to the more powerful foreign gods too, such as Littorn's Perkunas and Czernebog, Wotan Ammon of Cimberland, Brahma, the Sun. . . . Best not to chance their anger.'

'I see.'

Ap Ceorn offered cigars and matches. Van Sarawak inhaled and said querulously, 'Damn it, this would have to be a time line where they don't speak any language I know.' He brightened. 'But I'm pretty quick to learn, even without hypno. I'll get Deirdre to teach me.'

'You and me both,' said Everard in haste. 'But listen, Van.' He reported what he had learned.

'Hm.' The younger man rubbed his chin. 'Not so good, eh? Of course, if they'd just let us aboard our scooter, we could make an easy getaway. Why not play along with them?'

'They're not such fools,' answered Everard. 'They may believe in magic, but not in undiluted altruism.'

'Funny they should be so backward intellectually, and still have combustion engines.'

'No. It's quite understandable. That's why I asked about their religion. It's always been purely pagan; even Judaism seems to have disappeared, and Buddhism hasn't been very influential. As Whitehead pointed out, the medieval idea of one almighty God was important to the growth of science, by inculcating the notion of lawfulness in nature. And Lewis Mumford added that the early monasteries were probably responsible for the mechanical clock – a very basic invention – because of having regular hours for prayer. Clocks seem to have come late in this world.' Everard smiled wryly, a shield against the sadness within. 'Odd to talk like this. Whitehead and Mumford never lived.'

'Nevertheless —'

'Just a minute.' Everard turned to Deirdre. 'When was Afallon discovered?'

'By white men? In the year 4827.'

'Um . . . when does your reckoning start from?'

Deirdre seemed immune to further startlement. 'The creation of the world. At least, the date some philosophers have given. That is 5964 years ago.'

Which agreed with Bishop Ussher's famous 4004 BC, perhaps by sheer coincidence – but still, there was definitely a Semitic element in this culture. The creation story in Genesis was of Babylonian origin too.

'And when was steam (*pneuma*) first used to drive engines?' he asked.

'About a thousand years ago. The great Druid Boroihme O'Fiona —'

'Never mind.' Everard smoked his cigar and mulled his thoughts for a while before looking back at Van Sarawak.

'I'm beginning to get the picture,' he said. 'The Gauls were anything but the barbarians most people think. They'd learned a lot from Phoenician traders and Greek colonists, as well as from the Etruscans in cisalpine Gaul. A very energetic and enterprising race. The Romans, on the other hand, were a stolid lot, with few intellectual interests. There was little technological progress in our world till the Dark Ages, when the Empire had been swept out of the way.

'In *this* history, the Romans vanished early. So, I'm pretty sure, did the Jews. My guess is, without the balance-of-power effect of Rome, the Syrians did suppress the Maccabees; it was a near thing even in our history. Judaism disappeared and therefore Christianity never came into existence. But anyhow, with Rome removed, the Gauls got the supremacy. They started exploring, building better ships, discovering America in the ninth century. But they weren't so far ahead of the Indians that those couldn't catch up. . . . could even be stimulated to build empires of their own, like Huy Braseal today. In the eleventh century, the Celts began tinkering with steam engines. They seem to have got gunpowder too, maybe from China, and to have made several other inventions. But it's all been cut-and-try, with no basis of real science.'

Van Sarawak nodded. 'I suppose you're right. But what did happen to Rome?'

'I don't know. Yet. But our key point is back there somewhere.'

Everard returned his attention to Deirdre. 'This may surprise you,' he said smoothly. 'Our people visited this world about 2500 years ago. That's why I speak Greek but don't know what has occurred since. I would like to find out from you; I take it you're quite a scholar.'

She flushed and lowered long dark lashes such as few red-heads possess. 'I will be glad to help as much as I can.' With a sudden appeal: 'But will you help us in return?'

'I don't know,' said Everard heavily. 'I'd like to. But I don't know if we can.'

*Because, after all, my job is to condemn you and your entire world to death.*

## 5

When Everard was shown to his room, he discovered that local hospitality was more than generous. He was too tired and depressed to take advantage of it ... but at least, he thought on the edge of sleep, Van's slave girl wouldn't be disappointed.

They got up early here. From his upstairs window, Everard saw guards pacing the beach, but they didn't detract from the morning's freshness. He came down with Van Sarawak to breakfast, where bacon and eggs, toast and coffee added the last touch of dream. Ap Ceorn had gone back to town to confer, said Deirdre; she herself had put wistfulness aside and chattered gaily of trivia. Everard learned that she belonged to an amateur dramatic group which sometimes gave Classical Greek plays in the original; hence her fluency. She liked to ride, hunt, sail, swim – 'And shall we?' she asked.

'Huh?'

'Swim, of course?' Deirdre sprang from her chair on the lawn, where they had been sitting under flame-coloured leaves, and whirled innocently out of her clothes. Everard thought he heard a dull clunk as Van Sarawak's jaw hit the ground.

'Come!' she laughed. 'Last one in is a Sassenach!'

She was already tumbling in the grey surf when Everard and Van Sarawak shuddered their way down to the beach. The Venusian groaned. 'I come from a warm planet. My ancestors were Indonesians. Tropical birds.'

'There were some Dutchmen too, weren't there?' grinned Everard.

'They had the sense to move to Indonesia.'

'All right, stay ashore.'

'Hell! If she can do it, I can!' Van Sarawak put a toe in the water and groaned again.

Everard summoned up all the control he had ever learned and ran in. Deirdre threw water at him. He plunged, got hold of a slender leg, and pulled her under. They frolicked about for several minutes before running back to the house for a hot shower. Van Sarawak followed in a blue haze.

'Speak about Tantalus,' he mumbled. 'The most beautiful girl in the whole continuum, and I can't talk to her and she's half polar bear.'

Towelled dry and dressed in the local garb by slaves, Everard returned to stand before the living-room fire. 'What pattern is this?' he asked, pointing to the tartan of his kilt.

Deirdre lifted her ruddy head. 'My own clan's,' she answered. 'An honoured guest is always taken as a clan member during his stay, even if a blood feud is going on.' She smiled shyly. 'And there is none between us, Manslach.'

It cast him back into bleakness. He remembered what his purpose was.

'I'd like to ask you about history,' he said. 'It is a special interest of mine.'

She nodded, adjusted a gold fillet on her hair, and got a book from a crowded shelf. 'This is the best world history, I think. I can look up any details you might wish to know.'

*And tell me what I must do to destroy you.*

Everard sat down with her on a couch. The butler wheeled in lunch. He ate moodily, untasting.

To follow up his hunch – 'Did Rome and Carthage ever fight in war?'

'Yes. Two, in fact. They were allied at first, against Epirus, but fell out. Rome won the first war and tried to restrict Carthaginian enterprise.' Her clean profile bent over the pages, like a studious child. 'The second war broke out 23 years later, and lasted . . . hm . . . 11 years all told, though the last three were only a mopping up after Hannibal had taken and burned Rome.'

*Ah-hah!* Somehow, Everard did not feel happy at this success.

The Second Punic War (they called it the Roman War here) – or, rather, some crucial incident thereof – was the turning point. But partly out of curiosity, partly because he feared to tip his hand, Everard did not at once try to identify the deviation. He'd first have to get straight in his mind what had actually happened, anyway. (No ... what had not happened. The reality was here, warm and breathing beside him; he was the ghost.)

'So what came next?' he asked tonelessly.

'The Carthaginian empire came to include Hispania, southern Gaul, and the toe of Italy,' she said. 'The rest of Italy was impotent and chaotic, after the Roman confederacy had been broken up. But the Carthaginian government was too venal to remain strong. Hannibal himself was assassinated by men who thought his honesty stood in their way. Meanwhile, Syria and Parthia fought for the eastern Mediterranean, with Parthia winning and thus coming under still greater Hellenic influence than before.

'About a hundred years after the Roman Wars, some Germanic tribes overran Italy.' (That would be the Cimbri, with their allies the Teutones and Ambrones, whom Marius had stopped in Everard's world.) 'Their destructive path through Gaul had set the Celts moving too, eventually into Hispania and North Africa as Carthage declined. And from Carthage the Gauls learned much.

'A long period of wars followed, during which Parthia waned and the Celtic states grew. The Huns broke the Germans in middle Europe, but were in turn defeated by Parthia; so the Gauls moved in and the only Germans left were in Italy and Hyperborea.' (That must be the Scandinavian peninsula.) 'As ships improved, trade grew up with the Far East, both from Arabia and directly around Africa.' (In Everard's history, Julius Caesar had been astonished to find the Veneti building better vessels than any in the Mediterranean.) 'The Celtanians discovered southern Afallon, which they thought was an island – hence the "Ynys" – but they were thrown out by the Mayans. The Brittic colonies farther north did survive, though, and eventually won their independence.

'Meanwhile Littorn was growing apace. It swallowed up most of Europe for a while. The western end of the continent only regained its freedom as part of the peace settlement after the Hundred Years' War I've told you about. The Asian countries have shaken off their exhausted European masters and modernized themselves, while the Western nations have declined in their turn.' Deirdre looked up from the book, which she had been skimming as she talked. 'But this is only the barest outline, Manslach. Shall I go on?'

Everard shook his head. 'No, thanks.' After a moment: 'You are very honest about the situation of your own country.'

Deirdre said roughly, 'Most of us won't admit it, but I think it best to look truth in the eyes.'

With a surge of eagerness: 'But tell me of your own world. There is a marvel past belief.'

Everard sighed, switched off his conscience, and began lying.

The raid took place that afternoon.

Van Sarawak had recovered his poise and was busily learning the Afallonian language from Deirdre. They walked through the garden hand in hand, stopping to name objects and act out verbs. Everard followed, wondering vaguely if he was a third wheel or not, most of him bent to the problem of how to get at the scooter.

Bright sunlight spilled from a pale cloudless sky. A maple was a shout of scarlet, a drift of yellow leaves scudded across the grass. An elderly slave was raking the yard in a leisurely fashion, a young-looking guard of Indian race lounged with his rifle slung on one shoulder, a pair of wolfhounds dozed under a hedge. It was a peaceful scene; hard to believe that men prepared murder beyond these walls.

But man was man, in any history. This culture might not have the ruthless will and sophisticated cruelty of Western civilization; in fact, in some ways it looked strangely innocent. Still, that wasn't for lack of trying. And, in this world, a genuine science might never emerge, man might endlessly repeat the cycle of war, empire, collapse, and war. In Everard's future, the race had finally broken out of it.

For what? He could not honestly say that this continuum was worse or better than his own. It was different, that was all. And didn't these people have as much right to their existence as – as his own, who were damned to nullity if he failed?

He knotted his fists. The issue was too big. No man should have to decide something like this.

At the showdown, he knew, no abstract sense of duty

would compel him, but the little things and the little folk he remembered.

They rounded the house and Deirdre pointed to the sea. '*Awarlann*,' she said. Her loose hair burned in the wind.

'Now does that mean "ocean" or "Atlantic" or "water"?' laughed Van Sarawak. 'Let's go see.' He led her towards the beach.

Everard trailed. A kind of steam launch, long and fast, was skipping over the waves, a mile or two offshore. Gulls trailed it in a snowstorm of wings. He thought that, if he'd been in charge, a Navy ship would have been on picket out there.

Did he even have to decide anything? There were other Patrolmen in the pre-Roman past. They'd return to their respective eras and ...

Everard stiffened. A chill ran down his back and congealed in his belly.

They'd return, and see what had happened, and try to correct the trouble. If any of them succeeded, this world would blink out of space-time, and he would go with it.

Deirdre paused. Everard, standing in a sweat, hardly noticed what she was staring at, till she cried out and pointed. Then he joined her and squinted across the sea.

The launch was standing in close, its high stack fuming smoke and sparks, the gilt snake figurehead agleam. He could see the forms of men aboard, and something white, with wings. ... It rose from the poopdeck and trailed at the end of a rope, mounting. A glider! Celtic aeronautics had got that far, at least.

'Pretty,' said Van Sarawak. 'I suppose they have balloons too.'

The glider cast its tow and swooped inward. One of the guards on the beach shouted. The rest pelted from behind the house. Sunlight flashed off their guns. The launch headed straight for the shore. The glider landed, ploughing a furrow in the beach.

An officer yelled and waved the Patrolmen back. Everard had a glimpse of Deirdre's face, white and uncomprehending. Then a turret on the glider swivelled – a detached part of his mind guessed it was manually operated – and a light cannon spoke.

Everard hit the dirt. Van Sarawak followed, dragging the girl with him. Grapeshot ploughed hideously through the Afallonian soldiers.

There followed a spiteful crack of guns. Men sprang from the aircraft, dark-faced men in turbans and sarongs. *Hinduraj!* thought Everard. They traded shots with the surviving guards, who rallied about their captain.

That officer roared and led a charge. Everard looked up from the sand to see him almost upon the glider's crew. Van Sarawak leaped to his feet. Everard rolled over, caught him by the ankle, and pulled him down before he could join the fight.

'Let me *go*!' The Venusian writhed, sobbing. The dead and wounded left by the cannon sprawled nightmare red. The racket of battle seemed to fill the sky.

'No, you bloody fool! It's us they're after, and that wild Irishman's done the worst thing he could have —' A fresh outburst yanked Everard's attention elsewhere.

The launch, shallow-draught and screw-propelled, had run up into the shallows and was retching armed men. Too late the Afallonians realized that they had discharged their weapons and were now being attacked from the rear.

'Come on!' Everard hauled Deirdre and Van Sarawak to their feet. 'We've got to get out of here – get to the neighbours. . . .'

A detachment from the boat saw him and veered. He felt rather than heard the flat smack of a bullet into soil, as he reached the lawn. Slaves screamed hysterically inside the house. The two wolfhounds attacked the invaders and were gunned down.

Crouched, zigzag, that was the way: over the wall and out on to the road! Everard might have made it, but Deirdre stumbled and fell. Van Sarawak halted to guard her. Everard stopped also, and then it was too late. They were covered.

The leader of the dark men snapped something at the girl. She sat up, giving him a defiant answer. He laughed shortly and jerked his thumb at the launch.

'What do they want?' asked Everard in Greek.

'You.' She looked at him with horror. 'You two —' The officer spoke again. 'And me to translate. . . . No!'

She twisted in the hands that had closed on her arms, got

144

partly free and clawed at a face. Everard's fist travelled in a short arc that ended in a squashing of nose. It was too good to last. A clubbed rifle descended on his head, and he was only dimly aware of being frogmarched off to the launch.

6

The crew left the glider behind, shoved their boat into deeper water, and revved it up. They left all the guardsmen slain or disabled, but took their own casualties along.

Everard sat on a bench on the plunging deck and stared with slowly clearing eyes as the shoreline dwindled. Deirdre wept on Van Sarawak's shoulder, and the Venusian tried to console her. A chill noisy wind flung spindrift in their faces.

When two white men emerged from the deckhouse, Everard's mind was jarred back into motion. Not Asians after all. Europeans! And now when he looked closely, he saw the rest of the crew also had Caucasian features. The brown complexions were merely grease paint.

He stood up and regarded his new owners warily. One was a portly, middle-aged man of average height, in a red silk blouse and baggy white trousers and a sort of astrakhan hat; he was clean-shaven and his dark hair was twisted into a queue. The other was somewhat younger, a shaggy blond giant in a tunic sewn with copper links, legginged breeches, a leather cloak, and a purely ornamental horned helmet. Both wore revolvers at their belts and were treated deferentially by the sailors.

'What the devil?' Everard looked around once more. They were already out of sight of land, and bending north. The hull quivered with the haste of the engine, spray sheeted when the bows bit a wave.

The older man spoke first in Afallonian. Everard shrugged. Then the bearded Nordic tried, first in a completely un-recognizable dialect but afterwards: '*Taelan thu Cimbric?*'

Everard, who knew several Germanic languages, took a chance, while Van Sarawak pricked up his Dutch ears. Deirdre huddled back, wide-eyed, too bewildered to move.

'*Ja,*' said Everard, '*ein wenig.*' When Goldilocks looked un-certain, he amended it: 'A little.'

'*Ah, aen litt. Gode!*' The big man rubbed his hands. '*Ik hait*

*Boierik Wulfilasson ok main gefreond heer erran Boleslav Arkonsky.'*

It was no language Everard had ever heard of – couldn't even be the original Cimbric, after all these centuries – but the Patrolman could follow it reasonably well. The trouble came in speaking; he couldn't predict how it had evolved.

'What the hell arran thu maching, anyway?' he blustered. 'Ik bin aen man auf Sirius – the stern Sirius, mit planeten ok all. Set uns gebach or willen be der Teufel to pay!'

Boierik Wulfilasson looked pained and suggested that the discussion be continued inside, with the young lady for interpreter. He led the way back into the deckhouse, which turned out to include a small but comfortably furnished saloon. The door remained open, with an armed guard looking in and more on call.

Boleslav Arkonsky said something in Afallonian to Deirdre. She nodded, and he gave her a glass of wine. It seemed to steady her, but she spoke to Everard in a thin voice.

'We've been captured, Manslach. Their spies found out where you were kept. Another group is supposed to steal your travelling machine. They know where that is, too.'

'So I imagined,' replied Everard. 'But who in Baal's name are they?'

Boierik guffawed at the question and expounded lengthily his own cleverness. The idea was to make the Suffetes of Afallon think Hinduraj was responsible. Actually, the secret alliance of Littorn and Cimberland had built up quite an effective spy service. They were now bound for the Littornian embassy's summer retreat on Ynys Llangollen (Nantucket), where the wizards would be induced to explain their spells and a surprise prepared for the great powers.

'And if we don't do this?'

Deirdre translated Arkonsky's answer word for word: 'I regret the consequences to you. We are civilized men, and will pay well in gold and honour for your free co-operation. If that is withheld, we will get your forced co-operation. The existence of our countries is at stake.'

Everard looked closely at them. Boierik seemed embarrassed and unhappy, the boastful glee evaporated from him. Boleslav Arkonsky drummed on the tabletop, his lips compressed but a certain appeal in his eyes. *Don't make us do this. We have to live with ourselves.*

They were probably husbands and fathers, they must enjoy a mug of beer and a friendly game of dice as well as the next man, maybe Boierik bred horses in Italy and Arkonsky was a rose fancier on the Baltic shores. But none of this would do their captives a bit of good, when the almighty Nation locked horns with its kin.

Everard paused to admire the sheer artistry of this operation, and then began wondering what to do. The launch was fast, but would need something like twenty hours to reach Nantucket, as he remembered the trip. There was that much time, at least.

'We are weary,' he said in English. 'May we not rest awhile?'

'*Ja deedly*,' said Boierik with a clumsy graciousness. '*Ok wir skallen gode gefreonds bin, ni?*'

Sunset smouldering in the west, Deirdre and Van Sarawak stood at the rail, looking across a grey waste of waters. Three crewmen, their makeup and costumes removed, poised alert and weaponed on the poop; a man steered by compass; Boierik and Everard paced the quarterdeck. All wore heavy clothes against the wind.

Everard was getting some proficiency in the Cimbrian language; his tongue still limped, but he could make himself understood. Mostly, though, he let Boierik do the talking.

'So you are from the stars? These matters I do not understand. I am a simple man. Had I my way, I would manage my Tuscan estate in peace and let the world rave as it will. But we of the Folk have our obligations.' The Teutonics seemed to have replaced the Latins altogether in Italy, as the English had done the Britons in Everard's world.

'I know how you feel,' said the Patrolman. 'Strange that so many should fight when so few want to.'

'Oh, but this is necessary.' A near whine. 'Carthagalann stole Egypt, our rightful possession.'

'*Italia irredenta*,' murmured Everard.

'Hunh?'

'Never mind. So you Cimbri are allied with Littorn, and hope to grab off Europe and Africa while the big powers are fighting in the East.'

'Not at all!' said Boierik indignantly. 'We are merely asserting our rightful and historic territorial claims. Why, the king himself said . . .' And so on and so on.

Everard braced himself against the roll of the deck. 'Seems to me you treat us wizards rather hard,' he remarked. 'Beware lest we get really angered at you.'

'All of us are protected against curses and shapings.'

'Well —'

'I wish you would help us freely. I will be happy to demonstrate to you the justice of our cause, if you have a few hours to spare.'

Everard shook his head, walked off and stopped by Deirdre. Her face was a blur in the thickening dusk, but he caught a forlorn fury in her voice: 'I hope you told him what to do with his plans, Manslach.'

'No,' said Everard heavily. 'We are going to help them.'

She stood as if struck.

'What are you saying, Manse?' asked Van Sarawak.

Everard told him.

'No!' said the Venusian.

'Yes,' said Everard.

'By God, no! I'll —'

Everard grabbed his arm and said coldly: 'Be quiet. I know what I'm doing. We can't take sides in this world; we're against everybody, and you'd better realize it. The only thing to do is to play along with these fellows for a while. And don't tell that to Deirdre.'

Van Sarawak bent his head and stood for a moment, thinking. 'All right,' he said dully.


7

The Littornian resort was on the southern shore of Nantucket, near a fishing village, but walled off from it. The embassy had built in the style of its homeland; long, timber houses with roofs arched like a cat's back, a main hall and its outbuildings enclosing a flagged courtyard. Everard finished a night's sleep and a breakfast which Deirdre's eyes had made miserable by standing on deck as they came in to the private pier. Another, bigger launch was already there, and the grounds swarmed with hard-looking men. Arkonsky's excitement flared up as he said in Afallonian: 'I see the magic engine has been brought. We can go right to work.'

When Boierik interpreted, Everard felt his heart slam.

The guests, as the Cimbrian insisted on calling them, were led into an outsize room where Arkonsky bowed the knee to an idol with four faces, that Svantevit which the Danes had chopped up for firewood in the other history. A fire burned on the hearth against the autumn chill, and guards were posted around the walls. Everard had eyes only for the scooter, where it stood gleaming on the floor.

'I hear the fight was hard in Catuvellaunan to gain this thing,' remarked Boierik. 'Many were killed; but our gang got away without being followed.' He touched a handlebar gingerly. 'And this wain can truly appear anywhere its rider wishes, out of thin air?'

'Yes,' said Everard.

Deirdre gave him a look of scorn such as he had rarely known. She stood haughtily away from him and Van Sarawak.

Arkonsky spoke to her; something he wanted translated. She spat at his feet. Boierik sighed and gave the word to Everard:

'We wish the engine demonstrated. You and I will go for a ride on it. I warn you, I will have a revolver at your back. You will tell me in advance everything you mean to do, and if aught untoward happens, I will shoot. Your friends will remain here as hostages, also to be shot on the first suspicion. But I'm sure,' he added, 'that we will all be good friends.'

Everard nodded. Tautness thrummed in him; his palms felt cold and wet. 'First I must say a spell,' he answered.

His eyes flickered. One glance memorized the spatial reading of the position meters and the time reading of the clock on the scooter. Another look showed Van Sarawak seated on a bench, under Arkonsky's drawn pistol and the rifles of the guards. Deirdre sat down too, stiffly, as far from him as she could get. Everard made a close estimate of the bench's position relative to the scooter's, lifted his arms, and chanted in Temporal:

'Van, I'm going to try to pull you out of here. Stay exactly where you are now, repeat, exactly. I'll pick you up on the fly. If all goes well, that'll happen about one minute after I blink off with our hairy comrade.'

The Venusian sat wooden-faced, but a thin beading of sweat sprang out on his forehead.

'Very good,' said Everard in his pidgin Cimbric. 'Mount on the rear saddle, Boierik, and we'll put this magic horse through her paces.'

The blond man nodded and obeyed. As Everard took the front seat, he felt a gun muzzle held shakily against his back. 'Tell Arkonsky we'll be back in half an hour,' he instructed. They had approximately the same time units here as in his world, both descended from the Babylonian. When that had been taken care of, Everard said, 'The first thing we will do is appear in midair over the ocean and hover.'

'F-f-fine,' said Boierik. He didn't sound very convinced.

Everard set the space controls for ten miles east and a thousand feet up, and threw the main switch.

They sat like witches astride a broom, looking down on greenish-grey immensity and the distant blur which was land. The wind was high, it caught at them and Everard gripped tight with his knees. He heard Boierik's oath and smiled stiffly.

'Well,' he asked, 'how do you like this?'

'Why . . . it's wonderful!' As he grew accustomed to the idea, the Cimbrian gathered enthusiasm. 'Balloons are as nothing beside it. With machines like this, we can soar above enemy cities and rain fire down on them.'

Somehow, that made Everard feel better about what he was going to do.

'Now we will fly ahead,' he announced, and sent the scooter gliding through the air. Boierik whooped exultantly. 'And now we will make the instantaneous jump to your homeland.'

Everard threw the manoeuvre switch. The scooter looped the loop and dropped at a three-gee acceleration.

Forewarned, the Patrolman could still barely hang on. He never knew whether the curve or the dive had thrown Boierik. He only got a moment's glimpse of the man, plunging down through windy spaces to the sea, and wished he hadn't.

For a little while, then, Everard hung about the waves. His first reaction was a shudder. Suppose Boierik had had time to shoot? His second was a thick guilt. Both he dismissed, and concentrated on the problem of rescuing Van Sarawak.

He set the space verniers for one foot in front of the prisoners' bench, the time unit for one minute after he had departed. His right hand he kept by the controls – he'd have to work fast – and his left free.

*Hang on to your hats, fellahs. Here we go again.*

The machine flashed into existence almost in front of Van Sarawak. Everard clutched the Venusian's tunic and hauled him close, inside the spatiotemporal drive field, even as his right hand spun the time dial back and snapped down the main switch.

A bullet caromed off metal. Everard had a moment's glimpse of Arkonsky shouting. And then it was all gone and they were on a grassy hill sloping down to the beach. It was two thousand years ago.

He collapsed shivering over the handlebars.

A cry brought him back to awareness. He twisted around to look at Van Sarawak where the Venusian sprawled on the hillside. One arm was still around Deirdre's waist.

The wind lulled, and the sea rolled in to a broad white strand, and clouds walked high in heaven.

'Can't say I blame you, Van.' Everard paced before the scooter and looked at the ground. 'But it does complicate matters.'

'What was I supposed to do?' the other man asked on a raw note. 'Leave her there for those bastards to kill – or to be snuffed out with her entire universe?'

'Remember, we're conditioned. Without authorization, we couldn't tell her the truth even if we wanted to. And I, for one, don't want to.'

Everard glanced at the girl. She stood breathing heavily, but with a dawn in her eyes. The wind ruffled her hair and the long thin dress.

She shook her head, as if to clear it of nightmare, ran over and clasped their hands. 'Forgive me, Manslach,' she breathed. 'I should have known you'd not betray us.'

She kissed them both. Van Sarawak responded as eagerly as expected, but Everard couldn't bring himself to. He would have remembered Judas.

'Where are we?' she continued. 'It looks almost like Llangollen, but no dwellers. Have you taken us to the Happy Isles?' She spun on one foot and danced among summer flowers. 'Can we rest here a while before returning home?'

Everard drew a long breath. 'I've bad news for you, Deirdre,' he said.

She grew silent. He saw her gather herself.

'We can't go back.'

She waited mutely.

'The . . . the spells I had to use, to save our lives – I had no choice. But those spells debar us from returning home.'

'There is no hope?' He could barely hear her.

His eyes stung. 'No,' he said.

She turned and walked away. Van Sarawak moved to follow her, but thought better of it and sat down beside Everard. 'What'd you tell her?' he asked.

Everard repeated his words. 'It seems the best compromise,' he finished. 'I can't send her back to what's waiting for this world.'

'No.' Van Sarawak sat quiet for a while, staring across the sea. Then: 'What year is this? About the time of Christ? Then we're still upstairs of the turning point.'

'Yeh. And we still have to find out what it was.'

'Let's go back to some Patrol office in the farther past. We can recruit help there.'

'Maybe.' Everard lay down in the grass and regarded the sky. Reaction overwhelmed him. 'I think I can locate the key event right here, though, with Deirdre's help. Wake me when she comes back.'

She returned dry-eyed, though one could see she had wept. When Everard asked if she would assist in his own mission, she nodded. 'Of course. My life is yours who saved it.'

*After getting you into the mess in the first place.* Everard said carefully: 'All I want from you is some information. Do you know about . . . about putting people to sleep, a sleep in which they may believe anything they're told?'

She nodded doubtfully. 'I've seen medical Druids do that.'

'It won't harm you. I only wish to make you sleep so you can remember everything you know, things you believe forgotten. It won't take long.'

Her trustfulness was hard for him to endure. Using Patrol techniques, he put her in a hypnotic state of total recall and dredged out all she had ever heard or read about the Second Punic War. That added up to enough for his purposes.

Roman interference with Carthaginian enterprise south of the Ebro, in direct violation of treaty, had been the final rowelling. In 219 BC Hannibal Barca, governor of Carthaginian Spain, laid siege to Saguntum. After eight months he took it, and thus provoked his long-planned war with Rome. At the beginning of May, 218, he crossed the Pyrenees with 90,000 infantry, 12,000 cavalry, and 37 elephants, marched through Gaul, and went over the Alps. His losses en route were gruesome: only 20,000 foot and 6,000 horse reached Italy late in the year. Nevertheless, near the Ticinus River he met and broke a superior Roman force. In the course of the following year, he fought several bloodily victorious battles and advanced into Apulia and Campania.

The Apulians, Lucanians, Bruttians, and Samnites went over to his side. Quintus Fabius Maximus fought a grim guerrilla war, which laid Italy waste and decided nothing. But meanwhile Hasdrubal Barca was organizing Spain, and in 211 he arrived with reinforcements. In 210 Hannibal took and burned Rome, and by 207 the last cities of the confederacy had surrender to him.

'That's it,' said Everard. He stroked the coppery mane of the girl lying beside him. 'Go to sleep now. Sleep well and wake up glad of heart.'

'What'd she tell you?' asked Van Sarawak.

'A lot of detail,' said Everard. The whole story had required more than an hour. 'The important thing is this: her knowledge of those times is good, but she never mentioned the Scipios.'

'The who's?'

'Publius Cornelius Scipio commanded the Roman army at Ticinus. He was beaten there all right, in our world. But later he had the intelligence to turn westward and gnaw away the Carthaginian base in Spain. It ended with Hannibal being effectively cut off in Italy, and what little Iberian help could be sent him was annihilated. Scipio's son of the same name also held a high command, and was the man who finally whipped Hannibal at Zama; that's Scipio Africanus the Elder.

'Father and son were by far the best leaders Rome had. But Deirdre never heard of them.'

'So. . . .' Van Sarawak stared eastward across the sea, where Gauls and Cimbri and Parthians were ramping through the shattered Classical world. 'What happened to them in this time line?'

'My own total recall tells me that both the Scipios were at Ticinus, and very nearly killed. The son saved his father's life during the retreat, which I imagine was more like a stampede. One gets you ten that in *this* history the Scipios died there.'

'Somebody must have knocked them off,' said Van Sarawak. His voice tightened. 'Some time traveller. It could only have been that.'

'Well, it seems probable, anyhow. We'll see.' Everard looked away from Deirdre's slumbrous face. 'We'll see.'

8

At the Pleistocene resort – half an hour after having left it for New York – the Patrolmen put the girl in charge of a sympathetic Greek-speaking matron and summoned their colleagues. Then the message capsules began jumping through space-time.

All offices prior to 218 BC – the closest was Alexandria, 250–230 – were 'still' there, with 200 or so agents altogether. Written contact with the future was confirmed to be impossible, and a few short jaunts upstairs clinched the proof. A worried conference met at the Academy, back in the Oligocene Period. Unattached agents ranked those with steady assignments, but not each other; on the basis of his own experience, Everard found himself the chairman of a committee of top-bracket officers.

That was a frustrating job. These men and women had leaped centuries and wielded the weapons of gods. But they were still human, with all the ingrained orneriness of their race.

Everyone agreed that the damage would have to be repaired. But there was fear for those agents who had gone ahead into time before being warned, as Everard himself had done. If they weren't back when history was re-altered, they would never be seen again. Everard deputized parties to attempt rescue, but doubted there'd be much success. He warned them sternly to return within a day, local time, or face the consequences.

A man from the Scientific Renaissance had another point to make. Granted, the survivors' plain duty was to restore the 'original' time track. But they had a duty to knowledge as well. Here was a unique chance to study a whole new phase of humankind. Several years' anthropological work should be done before – Everard slapped him down with difficulty. There weren't so many Patrolmen left that they could take the risk.

Study groups had to determine the exact moment and circumstances of the change. The wrangling over methods went on interminably. Everard glanced out of the window, into the prehuman night, and wondered if the sabretooths weren't doing a better job after all than their simian successors.

When he had finally got his various gangs dispatched, he broke out a bottle and got drunk with Van Sarawak.

Reconvening next day, the steering committee heard from its deputies, who had run up a total of years in the future. A dozen Patrolmen had been rescued from more or less ignominious situations; another score would simply have to be written off. The spy group's report was more interesting. It seemed that two Helvetian mercenaries had joined Hannibal in the Alps and won his confidence. After the war, they had risen to high positions in Carthage. Under the names of Phrontos and Himilco, they had practically run the government, engineered Hannibal's murder, and set new records for luxurious living. One of the Patrolmen had seen their homes and the men themselves. 'A lot of improvements that hadn't been thought of in Classical times. The fellows looked to me like Neldorians, 205th millennium.'

Everard nodded. That was an age of bandits who had 'already' given the Patrol a lot of work. 'I think we've settled the matter,' he said. 'It makes no difference whether they were with Hannibal before Ticinus or not. We'd have hell's own time arresting them in the Alps without such a fuss that we'd change the future ourselves. What counts is that they seem to have rubbed out the Scipios, and that's the point we'll have to strike at.'

A nineteenth-century Britisher, competent but with elements of Colonel Blimp, unrolled a map and discoursed on his aerial observations of the battle. He'd used an infra-red telescope to look through low clouds. 'And here the Romans stood —'

'I know,' said Everard. 'A thin red line. The moment when they took flight is the critical one, but the confusion then also gives us our chance. Okay, we'll want to surround the battlefield unobtrusively, but I don't think we can get away with more than two agents actually on the scene. The baddies are going to be alert, you know, looking for possible counter-interference. The Alexandria office can supply Van and me with costumes.'

'I say,' exclaimed the Englishman, 'I thought I'd have the privilege.'

'No. Sorry.' Everard smiled with one corner of his mouth. 'No privilege, anyway. Just risking your neck, in order to negate a world full of people like yourself.'

'But dash it all —'

Everard rose. 'I've got to go,' he said flatly. 'I don't know why, but I've got to.'

Van Sarawak nodded.

They left their scooter in a clump of trees and started across the field.

Around the horizon and up in the sky waited a hundred armed Patrolmen, but that was small consolation here among spears and arrows. Lowering clouds hurried before a cold whistling wind, there was a spatter of rain; sunny Italy was enjoying its late fall.

The cuirass was heavy on Everard's shoulders as he trotted across blood-slippery mud. He had helmet, greaves, a Roman shield on his left arm and a sword at his waist; but his right hand gripped a stunner. Van Sarawak loped behind, similarly equipped, eyes shifting under the wind-ruffled officer's plume.

Trumpets howled and drums stuttered. It was all but lost among the yells of men and tramp of feet, screaming, riderless horses and whining arrows. Only a few captains and scouts were still mounted; as often before stirrups were invented, what started to be a cavalry battle had become entirely a fight on foot after the lancers fell off their mounts.

The Carthaginians were pressing in, hammering edged metal against the buckling Roman lines. Here and there the struggle was already breaking up into small knots, where men cursed and cut at strangers.

The combat had passed over this area already. Death lay around Everard. He hurried behind the Roman force, towards the distant gleam of the eagles. Across helmets and corpses, he made out a banner that fluttered triumphant red and purple. And there, looming monstrous against the grey sky, lifting their trunks and bawling, came a squad of elephants.

War was always the same: not a neat affair of lines across maps, nor a hallooing gallantry, but men who gasped and sweated and bled in bewilderment.

A slight, dark-faced youth squirmed nearby, trying feebly to pull out the javelin which had pierced his stomach. He was a slinger from Carthage, but the burly Italian peasant who sat next to him, staring without belief at the stump of an arm, paid no attention.

A flight of crows hovered overhead, riding the wind and waiting.

'This way,' muttered Everard. 'Hurry up, for God's sake! That line's going to break any minute.'

The breath was raw in his throat as he jogged towards the standards of the Republic. It came to him that he'd always rather wished that Hannibal had won. There was something repellent about the frigid, unimaginative greed of Rome. And here he was, trying to save the city. Well-a-day, life was often an odd business.

It was some consolation that Scipio Africanus was one of the few decent men left after the war.

Screaming and clangour lifted, and the Italians reeled back. Everard saw something like a wave smashed against a rock. But it was the rock which advanced, crying out and stabbing, stabbing.

He began to run. A legionary went past, howling his panic. A grizzled Roman veteran spat on the ground, braced his feet, and stood where he was till they cut him down. Hannibal's elephants squealed and blundered about. The ranks of Carthage held firm, advancing to an inhuman pulse of drums.

Up ahead, now! Everard saw men on horseback, Roman

officers. They held the eagles aloft and shouted, but nobody could hear them above the din.

A small group of legionaries trotted past. Their leader hailed the Patrolmen: 'Over here! We'll give 'em a fight, by the belly of Venus!'

Everard shook his head and continued. The Roman snarled and sprang at him. 'Come here, you cowardly....' A stun beam cut off his words. He crashed into the muck. His men shuddered, someone wailed, and the party broke into flight.

The Carthaginians were very near, shield to shield and swords running red. Everard could see a scar livid on the cheek of one man, the great hook nose of another. A hurled spear clanged off his helmet. He lowered his head and ran.

A combat loomed before him. He tried to go around, and tripped on a gashed corpse. A Roman stumbled over him in turn. Van Sarawak cursed and dragged him clear. A sword furrowed the Venusian's arm.

Beyond, Scipio's men were surrounded and battling without hope. Everard halted, sucked air into starved lungs, and looked into the thin rain. Armour gleamed wetly as a troop of Roman horsemen galloped closer, with mud up to their mounts' noses. That must be the son, Scipio Africanus to be, hastening to rescue his father. The hoofbeats made thunder in the earth.

'Over there!'

Van Sarawak cried out and pointed. Everard crouched where he was, rain dripping off his helmet and down his face. From another direction, a Carthaginian party was riding towards the battle around the eagles. And at their head were two men with the height and craggy features of Neldor. They wore GI armour, but each of them held a slim-barrelled gun.

'This way!' Everard spun on his heel and dashed towards them. The leather in his cuirass creaked as he ran.

The Patrolmen were close to the Carthaginians before they were seen. Then a horseman called the warning. Two crazy Romans! Everard saw how he grinned in his beard. One of the Neldorians raised his blast rifle.

Everard flopped on his stomach. The vicious blue-white beam sizzled where he had been. He snapped a shot, and one

of the African horses went over in a roar of metal. Van Sarawak stood his ground and fired steadily. Two, three, four –
and there went a Neldorian, down in the mud!

Men hewed at each other around the Scipios. The Neldorians' escort yelled with terror. They must have had the
blaster demonstrated beforehand, but these invisible blows
were something else. They bolted. The second of the bandits
got his horse under control and turned to follow.

'Take care of the one you potted, Van,' gasped Everard.
'Drag him off the battlefield – we'll want to question —' He himself scrambled to his feet and made for a riderless horse. He
was in the saddle and after the Neldorian before he was fully
aware of it.

Behind him, Publius Cornelius Scipio and his son fought
clear and joined their retreating army.

Everard fled through chaos. He urged speed from his
mount but was content to pursue. Once they had got out of
sight, a scooter could swoop down and make short work of
his quarry.

The same thought must have occurred to the time-rover.
He reined in and took aim. Everard saw the blinding flash
and felt his cheek sting with a near miss. He set his pistol to
wide beam and rode in shooting.

Another fire-bolt took his horse full in the breast. The
animal toppled and Everard went out of the saddle. Trained
reflexes softened the fall, he bounced to his feet and lurched
towards his enemy. The stunner was gone, fallen into the
mud, no time to look for it. Never mind, it could be salvaged
later, if he lived. The widened beam had found its mark; it
wasn't strong enough at such dilution to knock a man out,
but the Neldorian had dropped his blaster and the horse
stood swaying with closed eyes.

Rain beat in Everard's face. He slogged up to the mount.
The Neldorian jumped to earth and drew a sword. Everard's
own blade rasped forth.

'As you will,' he said in Latin. 'One of us will not leave this
field.'

9

The moon rose over mountains and turned the snow to a
sudden wan glitter. Far in the north, a glacier threw back the

light, and a wolf howled. The Cro-Magnons chanted in their cave, the noise drifted faintly through to the verandah.

Deirdre stood in darkness, looking out. Moonlight dappled her face and caught a gleam of tears. She stared as Everard and Van Sarawak came up behind her.

'Are you back so soon?' she asked. 'You only came here and left me this morning.'

'It didn't take long,' said Van Sarawak. He had got a hypno in Attic Greek.

'I hope —' she tried to smile – 'I hope you have finished your task and can rest from your labours.'

'Yes,' said Everard, 'we finished it.'

They stood side by side for a while, looking out on a world of winter.

'Is it true what you said, that I can never go home?' Deirdre spoke gently.

'I'm afraid so. The spells . . .' Everard swapped a glance with Van Sarawak.

They had official permission to tell the girl as much as they wished and take her wherever they thought she could live best. Van Sarawak maintained that that would be Venus in his century, and Everard was too tired to argue.

Deirdre drew a long breath. 'So be it,' she said. 'I'll not waste of life lamenting. But the Baal grant that they have it well, my people at home.'

'I'm sure they will,' said Everard.

Suddenly he could do no more. He only wanted to sleep. Let Van Sarawak say what had to be said, and reap whatever rewards there might be.

He nodded at his companion. 'I'm turning in,' he declared. 'Carry on, Van.'

The Venusian took the girl's arm. Everard went slowly back to his room.